Snake

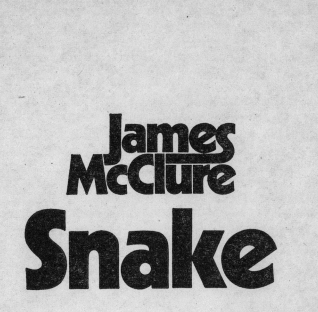

James McClure

Snake

PANTHEON BOOKS • NEW YORK

Manufactured in the United States of America
First Pantheon Paperback Edition

1

Eve defied death twice nightly, except on Sundays.

Sunday had just begun when there was a soft rap of knuckles on the dressing room door.

"Go away," she lisped, resentful.

Monday through Friday, she did a show at eleven and a show at one: the first timed to catch and hold the after-the-movies crowd; the second to prime them for their beds, titillated and eager to return for more. Come Saturday, however, both shows had to be over before the laws regarding public drinking and entertainment on the South African sabbath came into effect. Making a total of twelve hours in all, but it was tiring, stressful work.

So when her week ended on the stroke of midnight, she gladly turned into a pumpkin. Her taut orange skin and round face were just right for one, for a do-nothing, think-nothing, vegetating pumpkin which—once she had removed her small top plate—smiled gap-toothed into the mirror like a Halloween lantern. Nobody paid her to be pretty in private.

The knuckles rapped again.

Her smile quite disappeared. She replaced the plate and twisted round on her stool.

"Go on, *voetsak* you!" she called out with cold clarity. "Leave a girl in peace."

A shuffle of feet moving closer to the door.

"Eve?"

"That you, baby?"

"Can I see you for a minute, please?"

She had heard that one before, yet reached round for her gown and hitched it over her shoulders.

"You can see me from there," she said, opening the door a crack.

He really was a baby, a great big baby who just wanted

7

mothering—and, like a baby, was liable to kick up a terrible rumpus unless he got it.

"I wanted—do you think it's a hell of a cheek?"

"I'm listening."

She was also trying to work out what he was up to this time.

"Well," he said diffidently, bringing out a hand from behind him and showing her the champagne bottle grasped in it by the neck.

"Oh, ja?"

He offered her the bottle.

"It's all right," he said. "I don't have to come in."

She was obviously meant just to take it. But, what with clutching her gown across her bosom, she hadn't a hand to spare. And besides, that would have seemed mean.

"For me?"

"Please."

"Who gave you this idea? An old film?"

"I—I just thought of it."

"Oh, ja?"

"It's been a wonderful week."

"So you acted on impulse, hey?"

He smiled broadly, somehow flattered.

"That's me, Eve. I just wanted to—well—thank you and that. All right?"

Her instincts had cried wolf so often it had become impossible to make a fair assessment—one fair to him as well as to herself.

"You're on your own?"

"Sorry?"

"It's a big bottle."

"We don't have to—"

"Look," she said. "Just you wait a minute and I'll see."

She glanced down at his patent leather shoes. Neither tried to wedge the door. So she closed it gently and looked across into the big mirror. Her reflection was never much real company, and on this, her last night in Trekkersburg, the truth was she did feel a bit flat and lonely. On top of which, the spontaneity of the gesture had touched her. Nobody'd ever brought her champagne before, and she was close to a mood that hinted nobody else ever would.

"Okay, then?" she mouthed silently.

8

Her reflection raised an eyebrow that quivered, querying her judgment on the basis of the known facts—such as that big babies were always easy to kick out once she had had enough of them. Then it slowly regained its penciled symmetry. She shrugged. It shrugged.

"*Ach*, that's it," she said, fastening the belt of her gown properly.

Then she lifted a large wicker basket onto the divan and undid the leather straps. From inside it she took a python, roughly five feet long and almost two inches thick in the middle, beautifully patterned with light-brown shapes like round leaves, and draped him over her shoulders. The weight was that of a protective pair of arms.

He did a double take. It was usually the last she saw of the ones who weren't sincere.

"You don't mind?" she said. "Clint gets so restless after a show if I put him straight back in his basket. He'll be good."

His eyes gleamed. She took this for amusement, then was not sure, but by then he had politely sidled round her to take up a position beside where her street clothes hung from a hook.

Pressing the door closed behind her, she made certain it would stay shut against any other callers, and then pointed to the stool.

"Like a seat?"

"No, I'm fine, thanks—thank you very much."

"Well, I've been on my feet long enough for one day," she said, sitting down. "Glamorous, isn't it?"

She was getting in another dig about the way she had to live. The dressing room had three walls showing their brickwork through a thin coat of whitewash, a fourth wall made of bulging chipboard, an uneven cement floor, and a ceiling all stained and saggy like old underwear. As for furnishings, there was the blotchy mirror stuck crookedly to the wall opposite the door, a row of wire coat hangers on hooks for a wardrobe, a junkshop dressing table, a grass mat, a divan, and a wash basin with bad breath—plus, of course, the stool she was perched on, which gave you splinters if you weren't careful. No window at all.

"You are a bit untidy, Eve."

That was true, but one of those annoying surface remarks all the same.

9

"I bet where you live is worth keeping nice!" she said.

"That's a bit nasty! You don't really expect what film stars are given, do you? Although, mind, I'm not saying *you're* not worth it!"

"You trying to butter me up?"

"How?" he asked, in that abruptly innocent way of his.

"Ach, forget it. There's a glass and a mug by the basin."

"I should have thought to bring some!"

"You'll have to wash them. I use tissues for drying. Here—catch."

He fumbled his catch and dropped the box. Then made a dreadful clatter with the things in the basin. It gave her a certain amount of unkindly pleasure to see him doing such work. God, but he had a soft life.

The cork came out of the bottle with a sharp report. Snakes have no means of picking up airborne sound, but her sudden flinch caused the python to contract his coils, and she had to coax him out a little in order to stay comfortable. Very soon, once she was sure everything was as before, Clint could go back in his basket.

She was handed the more ladylike glass, filled to within a splash of the brim.

"To you, Eve!"

"Ta. And to you."

They drank.

"Is that your proper name? Eve?"

"Can you think of a better?"

He dimpled and shook his head.

"Put it this way," she added, finding she had almost downed the lot. "It's not what they'll put on my tombstone."

Why that sent a shudder through her as she said it was the booze for you. She was young, fit and healthy, and never really did anything dangerous.

"Goose walk over?" he asked, grinning.

"Pardon?"

"Too late! Not bad stuff—didn't know we had decent bubbly here. You and I should have started earlier on it."

He was beginning to assert himself. Beginning to feel more at home, perhaps, than he ever did in his own place, from what she had heard of it. The woman sounded a right bitch. Poor little chap.

"The whitewash will come off on your jacket."

10

"Oh, don't worry, I've got more—this isn't my only one."

She had noticed; a different suit practically every night—as if less-regular customers would ever notice.

"But let's talk about you for a change," he said. "Why not do more with yourself? Take this act to Lesotho and go the whole hog?"

"In front of *natives*? That'll be the day! Besides, what's this 'nude' rubbish? I thought you were the one who appreciated the psychological way I use—"

"Please, please. I was only wanting things better for you, the sort of—er—contracts you really deserve. You're a real artist and it's high time you realized it! What's Trekkersburg? There's a limit here on what it could ever do for you. And, I agree, the same applies really to Maseru. But have you ever thought of London? Hamburg? Vegas?"

"I see—and you could be my manager?"

"Why's this making you angry?"

"*Ach*, because every five minutes some bugger tries that lot of smoothie talk on me. I'm sick and tired of it!"

"Is that how it sounded?"

"Yes!"

"Then I'm sorry, really sorry to have said the wrong thing, although I promise you that I meant it. Come on, have another drop."

Typical. Do what you like, say sorry, and everything was fine again. All men stayed babies, when you came to think of it. Bit your finger and then went goo-goo. She was saddened but not surprised to find it all turning sour. Such was life.

But at least the champagne had not lost its sweetness. It must have cost a bomb retail. Sweet and tickly and gone in an instant down into a tummy kept empty for the more difficult positions. And from there, moving on to make her sore limbs feel better than a warm bath would have done, which the boardinghouse didn't seem to own anyway, and her head so pleasantly muzzy that the bare light no longer hurt her eyes.

She let him refill her glass.

"There—watch it doesn't spill! Can't let any go to waste. You know what I've decided to do? Take a little holiday on my own."

Plan B was being put into operation.

"Oh, ja?"

"Do you ever take a holiday?"

11

"Sometimes. When Clint has eaten a big meal."

His eyes became fixed on the python.

"Clint doesn't like being stared at," she said, then finished the line from her family show: "He thinks you're trying to hypnotize him."

He laughed loudly. "What does he feel like, Eve?"

"Smooth and nice—not slimy."

"How strong is he, really?"

"One his size can kill a duiker—even a buck much bigger. Touch him."

His free hand went into his pocket, and he raised the other to show it held the mug. Baby didn't want to.

"What's the matter—do you want your mummy?"

"That isn't like you, Eve," he said, very hurt.

Then the fingers, with their bitten-down nails, reached out and just dabbed at the scales. Clint tried to escape from her shoulders. She pulled him back.

"Not so cold," he said. "Super."

"Room temperature."

"I see. And you feed him on . . . ?"

"Guinea pigs."

"Dead or alive?"

"I just chuck them in his basket. Sometimes nothing happens for hours, then you hear the squeaking. Only I don't give him them often or he'd get even lazier. Wouldn't you, you old bastard?"

And she held the python's head with deceptive firmness as she nuzzled noses with him.

"Can I see him eat one?"

"Not feeding time."

"Please."

That was another of his magic words, like *sorry*.

"I'll pay for it. Clint can have one on the house, so to speak."

I'll pay.

"If you can tear yourself away from this club some night, come down and see us in Durban. I've got a spitting cobra that eats when he likes."

"Come off it, Eve! You know you're the real attraction!"

Double meanings next—he was doing well.

"Oh, ja? I fascinate you, do I?"

"Well, in a way, yes—yes, you do."

12

"And why?"

He shrugged, looking more thoughtful than she had expected.

"Because I play with snakes?"

"That might have been it to begin with—I thought it would be interesting talking to you—but I've also had this funny feeling. . . ."

His sentence seemed to quite genuinely tail off, and his eyes left her as he frowned and bit his thumbnail. There was a job for him in show business as well, no doubt of that.

"My God, you're not going to sulk, are you?" she said.

"Me?"

And he laughed softly, topping up her glass again, returning it to her with a flourish. The professional charm was switched on and off so suddenly you could almost hear the click.

"What exactly did you want to thank me for? I get paid for doing it, don't I?"

"You. Your show. All of it."

"Turns you on?"

"Does someone I know."

"Hey! This is something new! Don't tell me you've actually got a girlfriend hidden someplace?"

"Oh, she's not here. She's—she's on holiday."

"*Ach,* I realize that she isn't standing outside the door, man. I was just surprised because, after what you've told me, it hardly seems likely that your old battleship would approve."

"I never take her home with me," he said solemnly.

"Hell! As bad as that, is it?"

He laughed longer than she did.

Sick, that, him wanting to watch Clint gobble up a guinea pig. Things were now taking a little time to sink in, which was also nice. She'd never watched, even though it was just a fact of life like any other. Clint had to eat, but nobody had to see him do it. Most people would think the same way she did, so he couldn't be all that typical. He was weird.

"Are you weird?" she asked, sipping a little more.

"What a question!"

"I was thinking about you wanting to gawk at Clint having his num-nums."

"I'd just be interested. What's weird in that?"

13

Nothing, when you thought about how excited the same thing would make small kids. If they saw it happen in a game reserve, they'd love it and show no pity or other inside things. If the snake came for them, that would be a different matter, but their fear—like his—was an outside one. And she saw that happening all around her every night to grownups.

"What are you dreaming about?" he asked, making his voice friendly but not quite covering his nervousness.

"I was thinking."

"Is it catching?"

As if able to read her mind, he reached out again to touch the python.

"Not too close to his head," she warned.

"Pythons don't bite."

"Who told you that?"

"But they're not poisonous."

"Blood poisoning. You can catch blood poisoning from his teeth—they're dirty."

He winced. "Can't it go in the basket?"

"Just now."

So the girlfriend was away. Oh, yes, that began to explain a few things. Such as a bottle of champagne so big that two people could get very drunk on it. A bottle that had probably been shown to quite a few eyes in the club earlier on, and there had also probably been jokes about her. Even a few coarse bets laid. It was becoming clearer.

"You haven't been to my dressing room before," she said.

"I know. So?"

"It wasn't so private at the table."

"What—what are you hinting at?"

Quick as a flash, he was. Look at the innocent smile.

"You told your friends you were coming here?"

"What?"

"Friends, pals, closest buddies."

He frowned, as if he didn't understand.

"Am I right?"

"I don't really have any," he said. "Certainly nobody I'd tell this to."

Tell this to.

She hesitated. This was the moment to kick him out. Yet she could still be the loser: he could go back and make up something filthy for his cronies that would have them all out-

14

side, banging on the door, waving bottles. Or waiting for her in the alley, or tailing her back to the boardinghouse. The bugger of it was she had allowed him to stay too long already, and so kicking him out wasn't going to solve anything. If only there was some way she could stop him from telling anyone stories that could hurt her—make him run off home with his tail between his legs. If only . . .

There was a way! And by the time she had finished with him, he wouldn't even want to think about it, let alone talk. She knew men.

"Equal shares," she demanded.

"It's not making you too . . . y'know?"

"Gives me funny feelings."

He cocked his head at that, broadening his smile. Then concentrated on getting that extra bit more into her glass.

She adjusted Clint's position, and her gown began to slip open in the front. She let it fall how it pleased, aware her bosom was gradually pushing out. Soon both patches would be catching the light.

"What sort of funny feelings?" he asked. "Do you think they're like mine?"

"How should I know?"

"I—I can't put mine into words," he said.

"Nor mine either," she said, letting her knees slowly part.

He gulped down what was left in his mug. Sweat seeped onto his brow. It must have felt like a wet dream coming true.

Her breasts were out. Round and full, but not so heavy she got a heat rash under them, as some did. Tanned a deep orange like the rest of her. Every bit.

"Something embarrassing you?"

"No!" He looked away.

Again, she knew what to do. She pulled Clint's head around and guided him to slide down off her shoulders, parting her cleavage. This made the adhesive prickle and the patches feel as if they might pop off.

"Christ," he said, staring.

She took Clint and redirected him so that he eased back up around her neck, his tongue flickering soft against her skin, his two little feet scratching as he twisted and used his belly scales. She moved as sensuously as the snake did, work-

15

ing him into a comfortable position, and then she held him there.

"I told you about staring," she murmured.

"You actually . . . I mean, you really do get a . . ."

"Isn't that why you came round here tonight?"

"No, I didn't . . ."

"The show? Didn't turn you on, too? Or is it only us girls?"

Clint was heading down between her breasts, running a sleek chin over her hard little belly. She let him think he was getting away, then clamped his head tight in her thighs, halting his slither, for just a second.

He went pale.

"Do you like the encore, baby?" she asked, parting her legs and allowing Clint to gain the floor. The python naturally went straight under the dressing table.

"Pardon?" he said, coming down off tiptoe.

"Does he make you feel jealous?" she asked, lolling back, an elbow in a mess of spilled powder. "That's what most of them say. That Clint makes them jealous. Green, that's the color they go."

He took a pace toward her and then said, "Will it stay there?"

"My feelings are getting even funnier."

"But will the snake . . . ?"

"He'll come if I whistle."

"Will you?"

"What?" she asked, making her smile dirty.

The gown slipped from her shoulders. She stood, ankles well apart, hands on hips, then began humming an opening number, lifting one shoulder at him and then the other.

His eyes darted from her to the floor and back.

"Touch," she invited.

He saw her mouth pout to whistle.

"Come on, it's not cold," she said. And whistled very softly.

He started back. "Jesus, Eve . . ."

She began thrusting with her hips, jiggling her bosom, but all very slowly and in time to the soft, soft whistle.

Then turned her mouth into a big, welcoming smile.

His hand reached out for her, but she swayed back, teasingly. To touch her, he would have to take another step for-

16

ward. He looked at the foot of the dressing table, as if measuring the distance with his eye.

"What's the matter, baby? Haven't you got?"

And she imitated the rearing action of her other pet, spreading her hand like a hood, and laughing at how funny this was. Which rather shocked her.

"For Christ's sake!"

He was pointing behind her. Clint must have peeped his head out.

"Oh, so that's what turns you on? I've got one like a little apple!"

Old gags always found their uses. And she turned, standing now with her ankles together, and smiled at him over her shoulder. While tightening one thigh muscle and then the other, knowing this would make her bottom bunch and bounce.

Bunch and bounce.

He had to. He started toward her. She raised her arms slightly so that he could slip his hands around and cup her, squeeze her, grab her.

As his sweating palms brushed her sides, she bent forward and dragged Clint out by the tail so his underneath rasped on the floor. This hurt him and he hissed.

Behind her, kitchy-coo nearly fell over himself.

"Eve, for God's sake, put it in the basket!"

She tugged at the bow on her bikini, removed the patches rather painfully, and confronted him again, with the python once more over her shoulders, hanging like a tape measure.

"Come—and get it," she said.

"This isn't—"

"*Ach*, don't keep Clinty boy waiting, baby—he wants to jump into his own beddy, too."

"And—"

She nodded at the divan.

"All clothesy-wosies neatly folded!"

His dilemma was a knockout.

Up went the hands to his bow tie, but Clint's head followed the movement, and they dropped away, shaking. She managed to get a hand to the basket and flipped back its lid. He started to tug his clothes off and a shirt button went *ping* against the wash basin without him noticing because he never took his eyes off her. Not once.

17

"I'm ready!"

"Look, Clint," she giggled.

He glanced down at himself, over the slight potbelly, and saw nothing was happening.

"Oh, Jesus . . ."

"You'll just have to show him, Clint, won't you? Or Eve's going to be a very frustrated lady."

The python went into the routine as if he knew it, but took his cues from the light touches she gave as her fingers fluttered and fondled. Clint was really a very, very dumb animal, but all the more lovable for it.

"It must be the snake!" he said. "This has never—"

"You're not impotent, are you, my sweet? Not leading a girl on for nothing?"

"Perhaps it's because I've never thought of you this—"

"Do I remind you of your mother?" She laughed.

There was the gleam again.

"What you're doing to me isn't bloody funny," he pleaded.

His additional little problem had not been part of her plan—it was possibly as much of a surprise to her—but it was well worth cultivating. She brought Clint up from the front way, taking ages over it and watching its effect.

She must have overdone the last bit, because the problem suddenly disappeared.

"You're really ready, then, my sweet?"

"*Eve,*" he begged in a whisper.

"Let's make it an orgy, hey? The three of us?"

She had also dropped her voice very low.

"Please! I'll pay anything. Just—"

That was the moment.

"Pay? It's free! Come on!"

He stepped urgently toward her, stopping short.

How she laughed. Rocked and wheezed and pouted kisses. Laughed and laughed. Very softly, laughed and laughed. Staggered a little, too, and had to wind Clint once around her neck for him to stay aboard. Which brought on a coughing fit.

"Whore!" he snarled at her.

"Worm!" she retorted.

"I want!"

"I don't—not with you, baby."

"I will!"

"No, you bloody won't!"

All this in whispers still.

"You think I'm scared?"

"Huh! I can *see* you are!" And she stuck out her tongue at him.

Pa had always cautioned that one day she would go too far with one of her acts. Do something to a man she wouldn't believe possible.

Or upset a snake so much it would forget its manners and be forced to take advantage.

As she lay strangling in a scarlet hurricane on the floor of the dressing room, she had to agree, for the first time in her life, that the no-good old drunkard had been right about one thing.

Then her top plate fell out and she grimaced up at the ceiling like a Halloween lantern. One in which a candle guttered briefly before the pumpkin turned a dull rust color, all mottled and nasty.

2

Monday morning in the morgue was hell for some, heaven for others.

The NCO normally in charge, Van Rensberg, was on sick leave after an industrial accident—as the compensation papers called it—that had given him septicemia, and his place had been reluctantly taken by Sergeant Jacobus Kloppers, recently returned from Rhodesia's northern border.

Kloppers was having adjustment problems. First to the idea of being out of the firing line, which he had secretly not enjoyed, and then to the fact that his previous billet had been usurped by a Jew. He wasn't particularly anti-Semitery, or whatever the word was, but it remained inescapably the Jewishness of the bloke that was causing the trouble. It didn't seem long since he had seen a story in the papers saying: FIRST JEWISH RECRUIT GRADUATES AT POLICE COLLEGE, and now Trekkersburg had one all to themselves, with more press pictures to prove it. JEWISH CONSTABLE IN CHARGE OF BOOK OF LIFE, said the headline on a clipping his wife had posted to him, while the caption had been a lot of rubbish about loving your country whoever you were. But seeing that all white citizens had their Book was a most responsible job, Kloppers had argued on his return, not something to be left to a rookie. His superiors, however, whose enthusiasm for the new regulation had always seemed suspect to him, hadn't seen it that way. Any fool could supervise personal particulars, they told him, not that Oppenheimer was anything like a fool, only very junior, and what they needed desperately, higher up, was a seasoned man good at paper work. Yes, hopefully as good at it as he was, and willing to work in quiet surroundings, largely on his own for most of the time. In effect, the candidate would be virtually in charge of a department. An important one. Run it his own way. Would he

20

take it? Good! A very wise move. Only he must be careful and always wear his rubber gloves. . . .

The bastards.

It wasn't the Book of Life he held in his hands. Just the opposite, and woefully short on personal particulars it was, too. In fact, Kloppers couldn't even put a name to half his problems, and had given them labels marked with the letters of the alphabet for the time being.

They were everywhere. The fridge had been full by Saturday night, and so all four tables had been used up, with the leftovers going in the sink—two babies, Bantu—and on trays on the floor.

Kloppers felt again the mild panic he had known when given his first filing job in the office of a very untidy lieutenant. He just didn't know where to start. But he did know there was far too much for the district surgeon to get through in one morning, and he'd have to arrange some sort of order of priority. There were no whites among them, so bang went his first theory. He could try going on down through the classes of citizenship—Colored, Indian, and Bantu—but that seemed like splitting hairs. He could, of course, divide them according to whether death was suspicious or accidental. Yes, that was it. Providing he could tell . . . Man, it was going to be a bugger. A nightmare. And Dr. Christiaan Strydom was bound to come chuckling in very shortly.

"*Ach*, start with A," he mumbled to himself, leaving his stuffy little office and almost tripping over K.

While his black assistant, N2134 Nxumalo, sat outside in the sun and baked comfortably in his constable's uniform, charging up warmth against the chill indoors, and much enjoying this unprecedentedly slow start to the day. A great advantage of his position was that he was believed incapable of any initiative, and was expected to wait until he had been told what to do. Usually, old Sarge Van Rensberg would have had him running round in circles by now, threatening to take the bone cutters to his *tondo* if he didn't get down out of his bloody tree and do some work.

"You's a idle kaffir!" Nxumalo mimicked fondly, shaking his head at the memory of their four years together. Now, when this one could justly call him an idle kaffir, he didn't. Mad!

And bad at his job, which Nxumalo felt he could have

done blindfolded. Still, that was not his worry.

Nxumalo coughed and sneezed. The consequence of trying to laugh with a lungful of smoke. The funniest thing about his new boss, Kloppers, was that he obviously thought the weekend was over. That there would not be any more bodies landing on the doorstep to spoil his lovely lists. Whereas there would have to be one at least, if not two or half a dozen, to add to his troubles before nightfall.

He would see. It was the way.

His name had been Songqoza Sishanagane Shepstone Siyayo. Everyone called him Lucky. He was dead. Not all of him, but enough for a working definition.

If his blood still moved, this was thanks to gravitation rather than circulation, and the mass of cells still alive would be getting the news by and by, so it was only a matter of time. Although, with their communications center all shot to hell, this would possibly amount to no more than grim rumor before their own sudden disintegration began. Dust to dust, potassium to potassium.

Lucky's other dependents were, however, being informed directly of his murder. And asked to come down without delay to the small store off the Peacevale road. Where parts of them would die also. Because, as swiftly as the bullet traveled, it would nonetheless take a little while to get around to them all and realize fully its powers of destruction.

Lieutenant Tromp Kramer of the Trekkersburg Murder and Robbery Squad straightened up, popped another peppermint into his mouth, and backed off three paces.

Death was never pretty, but this time it came damn close to it.

Lucky had died against the shelves that held his stock of sweets, up near the single dusty display window where the light was good. Now that the torn canvas awning had been raised, this light came pure and unimpeded from the sky and, by way of reflection, off the glaring dirt road and the paintwork of the two vehicles parked outside, to put a sparkle into each wide-mouthed glass jar.

By narrowing the eyes, a variety of colorful impressions was possible. The most strongly suggested of these—if the least appropriate—seemed the gem-studded wall of a fairytale cavern.

22

It was all there, from the uncut glow of fruit gums to pink pearls of sugar-coated peanuts, silver nuggets of foil-wrapped nougat, amber slabs of toffee brittle, jade lozenges in lemon and lime flavors, and, spilled out below, the penny trappings of playground sovereignty: lollipop scepters and a great wealth of gold coins.

Over which twinkled a prodigious scattering of rock-candy diamonds and hard-boiled emeralds—and as many, if not more, blood rubies so thickly strewn that only the smallest pendants no longer glistened.

Amid which sprawled, like the errant guardian of a treasure trove who had just nodded off, a brightly dressed figure in brown sandals. The peppermints lay over him like a gentle fall of peach blossoms.

In the ten minutes, Lucky's skin color had lightened from plain to milk chocolate, he had begun to give off a sickly smell, and the surprised expression on his face had almost completely melted away.

"Christ, ja, but it's hot," said Kramer, turning to the white sergeant in khaki overalls at his side. The grease marks on the man's flat, solid features made him think of a workshop manual.

"Not so lucky—hey, Lieutenant?"

"Better than cancer."

"They get cancer?"

"Uh-huh."

"Man, you live and learn."

"Don't bet on it," Kramer murmured dryly, confirmed in a belief that Bokkie Howells owed everything to heredity, including his engineering genius—same as a weaver bird. "Now back to business. What if—"

"The gun, sir—thirty-two or thirty-eight?"

"Eight. Bull's-eye at close range."

"Not two shots?" queried Bokkie, pointing.

"That's the exit wound."

"And you say it's the same method as before?"

"Uh-huh. Number five. Till cleaned out. Car used for getaway. Talking of same, what about my shocks, then? How long will it take?"

Bokkie was from the police garage; the pair of them had been road-testing Kramer's new Chev Commando when the

23

call to Peacevale came through. The suspension was altogether too soft for dirt.

"Could have it ready for you by tomorrow, say five
o'clock."

"Two days for four shocks?"

"Have a heart, sir. Got to order the spares. Make out the
requisitions. Hey, he's starting to pee in his pants."

"It's legal."

"Could try—and I mean try, mark you—to get something
done by tonight. But I'd have to take it now."

"Fine with me. Uniformed has put up roadblocks, and
Zondi is here anyway with his own vehicle. You go when you
want."

The sergeant seemed in no hurry. He looked around the
store and then out over the heads of the crowd at the shanties
ranged opposite.

"Not much of a place," he sniffed.

"True," agreed Kramer, glancing at his watch.

"Can't have been much in the till either, this being a
Monday."

"Uh-huh."

Kramer picked up an interesting piece of mud, which bore
the clear imprint of an unusual rubber sole. The damned
thing proved within seconds to have come off the dead man's
left sandal.

"Five in two weeks is bad," Bokkie conceded, "but they
must have all been in Peacevale—haven't seen a thing about
them in the papers. What's so special?"

Irritation made Kramer bite through the dissolving peppermint and hurt his tongue.

"The papers?" he snapped, tasting blood. "Reporters?
Those bastards can't see what's under their noses—and their
values, so called, are all up to *kak!*"

Bokkie flinched. He could be an insensitive sod in many
ways, and intellectual words were wasted on him, but his ear
never missed a grated gear change.

"Hey, sir, I didn't mean to—"

"What's news to them? You tell me. Another coon killed in
Peacevale? Hell, no. That happens all the time—that's not
news. But let a Monday Clubber lift a bottle of sherry in a
supermarket, and they bloody crucify her on headlines so
wide." Kramer lifted his arms.

24

"Fair's fair, sir. They do put wog death sentences in—I've seen them."

"Ja, I know, death sentence—that's a good description for it. Can't you see, man? Or are you making the same mistake?"

"Not feeling sorry enough for the coons, Lieutenant?"

"Christ, no! In thinking it's two worlds apart. That what happens in one doesn't mean anything in the other. They actually *touch*, don't they?"

"But so far—"

"Exactly—that's the whole point I'm trying to make. So far these bastards haven't tried elsewhere. But they're bloody black lightning, man! Bang, in-out, no description, no sod all. How long do you think it will take before they catch on and move where the money is?"

"Hell," said Bokkie, deeply impressed by such elementary foresight. "It's a race against time, then, sir?"

"Uh-huh," replied Kramer, looking down again at one of the losers. Lucky and he had been friends.

The emergency service put the call through to the duty officer at ten-thirty sharp. He noted the time on his pad and the other essentials. When he had enough, he put the receiver down.

"Bloody hell," he said to his fishing companion, who had wandered across from Housebreaking, "but that bloke was doing his nut. Got a girl strangled."

"Oh, ja? Big deal."

"*Ach,* no—he meant a *girl* girl. Y'know—a white female, young."

"Hey? Where?"

"The Wam-bam."

"Don't get it."

"Wam-bam, thank you, ma'am. Monty's place."

"Then I'm not surprised. Going to tell the lieutenant? He'll also do his nut! They say this Peacevale gang have got him by the shorts and he just doesn't want to know."

"Sorry, but he'll have to—colonel's out."

"What about Sarge Marais?"

"I'll tell him, don't worry, but first his superior has to be informed. All in standing orders. Besides, it's a pleasure to screw the bastard for once."

25

"That's more like it," said his fishing companion.
And they laughed.

Bokkie Howells doubled back to pick up Kramer after the message came through. Then he drove him into town with a respect for moving parts that was agonizing. Even a donkey cart on the approach road to the divided highway managed to beat them across the line.

Peacevale petered out in a straggle of lopsided homes and black pedestrians trudging the shoulder. The high security fences guarding the gray railway yards gradually gave way to the whitewash and white folk of the old part of Trekkersburg, wire gates and palm trees; then slowly the concrete of the tall administration buildings took over, as sharp as paper cutouts against the flat blue sky.

They entered the city center down a wide street along which three black delivery men were jockeying their motorcycles for position.

"Bloody menace," grumbled Bokkie, abandoning his droned speculation about the dead girl's morals. "They should never have taken them off their bikes. There—you see?"

The leading motorcycle struck a car that suddenly swung out of a parking area, sending the rider bouncing on his crash helmet, with his load of booze bottles after him.

Kramer caught a glimpse of a pregnant housewife pinned by shock in the driving seat of her Mini.

"That'll teach you, boy!" yelled Bokkie, as they sedately negotiated the obstacle. "Teach you how to bloody behave on the road!"

He was so enormously gratified by this chance demonstration of a pet theory that he overshot the address clipped to the dashboard.

So Kramer reached for the handbrake, jerked it on hard, and got out to more squeals and the blare of outraged horns.

"See you," he said, and walked away.

"Where's the district surgeon?" Kloppers demanded, as though Nxumalo had inadvertently stacked him in a corner.

"Me, I don't know, boss."

"Being late like this isn't funny! Said he'd be here sharp at quarter to, and look at the time now. Plus where has Fingerprints got to? He should have been here to take snaps of the unidentified. They've got one more minute or I get on that phone."

"*Hau,* shame."

"And you? What have you been doing for the last half hour?"

"Nothing, boss."

"Good. I've got enough worries as it is."

The narrow alleyway ran between a shoe shop and a real estate agency, ending in a high red brick wall made more interesting by exterior plumbing.

Halfway down it, Kramer stopped outside a door painted with bright zigzags under a neon sign on the lintel that read THE WIGWAM. On one side in a glass case were some poor prints of a female playing with snakes. She was not worth more than one look.

He went in and found himself shoulder deep in the press. The photographer from the *Trekkersburg Gazette* had better sense than to raise his camera, but some long-haired baboon took a shot of him.

"Film," said Kramer, holding out his hand.

"Sorry?"

"Film," Kramer repeated, snapping his fingers.

"Ah, come on," he whined. "Cool it, man—okay?"

"Right, charge him with obstruction," Kramer said to a pale-cheeked constable who had just heaved himself into view. "And get the rest out onto the street. What the hell are they doing here?"

Before pausing to hear another word from anyone, he shoved his way through and went down into the club. The main area, with its tatty décor of supposedly Red Indian origin, which included headdresses made with fowl feathers, hinted at a midnight massacre. All the chairs had their legs in the air, and there was a lingering stink of smoke and the armpit war.

But no actual body.

Kramer picked up an empty wine bottle and rattled a spoon against it for attention.

"Who's that?" a sharp voice challenged from somewhere.

"The bloody cavalry, man—what do you think?"

The red curtains at the back of the small stage parted and

27

a proportionately small man, the color and consistency of an unbaked bun, made his entrance in the neatest way possible. His casual clothes were so formally pleated they probably still had a pin left in them, and his curly black goatee looked like a graft from the groin.

Kramer felt a prejudice forming.

"Get this straight: I'm Mr. Monty Stevenson and I'm the manager of this club. These are *my* premises! And if I've told you once, the Sunday *News* has the exclu—"

"Kramer, Murder and Robbery Squad."

Gulp, went the silk cravat.

"The lieutenant?"

"Uh-huh."

Stevenson advanced hesitantly across the boards, his built-up shoes clicking loudly.

"I do apologize, but I thought they were going to tell you not to bother after all. I let them use my phone in the office."

"Why's that? Is this a hoax?"

"Heavens, no! But your doctor said—"

"The DS? Is he here?"

"Er, yes. In the dressing room, the scene of the tragedy. Would you like me to show you the way?"

"You'd better!" growled Kramer.

He followed after him past a notice warning NO ADMITTANCE TO MEMBERS—STRICTLY PRIVATE and soon saw the reason why. The dim passage beyond the velvet hangings was a disgrace of squashed cockroaches and splintered floorboards. They clattered up a short flight of steps, took a left turn, and halted at a closed door with a paper star stuck to it.

Stevenson raised a hand to knock, but Kramer pushed him aside.

"That's fine," he said. "Now you get back to your office and see that if there's a call for me from Peacevale, I get to hear about it."

"Gladly," the manager said, and tip-tapped off.

Then the door was opened from the inside and Dirk Gardiner, a warrant officer from Fingerprints, stuck his crew cut out to see what the noise was about.

"Oh, sh—sugar," he said.

"So this is where you've been hiding, you bastard!"

"Look, Lieutenant, I was on my way when I got called here. Haven't even been to the mortuary yet."

"You're boasting, or what?"

"Be with you in a tick," replied Gardiner, as good-naturedly as ever. He had enough muscle under his blue safari suit to treat the world in the way he expected it to treat him. And somehow it worked.

"Guess who's arrived?" chuckled Strydom from within. "But don't start yelling at us, hey? We got a message for you not to come out to the duty officer soon as we could. You see him about it."

Kramer's brow creased.

"Ja, it's just a fatal," Gardiner explained, winding on another frame in his Pentax. "Stevenson, the stupid bastard, reported he'd found a girlie strangled. Didn't explain properly, says he was in a hell of a state. All shocked and—"

He stepped placidly aside to avoid being trampled underfoot.

Strydom, as gnomelike as ever, was kneeling in his new plastic apron—from which his wife had cut the frilly bits—beside a python with its head bashed in, making careful use of his tape measure. At his elbow was a corpse with red eyeballs, speckled skin, and arms folded demurely on its chest under a dressing gown.

"Oh, her," said Kramer.

"Sonja Bergstroom, alias Eve. Got careless and had an accident. Put up a hell of a fight, though. Should see the grazes she got from the concrete."

"Who's in charge here?"

"Sergeant Marais," said Gardiner. "Gone to the bog a moment."

"And he's happy?"

"Should be by now."

"Hey?"

"Sorry, sir. Yes, quite satisfied."

"Fascinating," murmured Strydom, taking another prod at the broad marks on the corpse's neck. "I must see if I can't put a little paper together. Get the snake park in Durban to help me."

"Ja, must be a moral in it, too, Doc."

"Wam-bam," suggested Kramer. The novelty had worn off.

"What's that, Trompie?"

"Mr. Gardiner here has urgent business in Peacevale.

29

Tell Marais I'll see him later. Okay?"

"Sounds ominous," Strydom said, smiling somewhere in his Santa Claus beard, and beginning to coil the snake into a white plastic bag. "What a shambles today has been."

Which proved an understatement once Kramer got back to Lucky's store. There two very distressed Bantu constables were obliged to inform him that while they had been keeping the onlookers at bay round the front, two youths had sneaked into the premises from the back.

"It was I who observed these *tsotsis* making off with their ill-gotten gains," chipped in the minister from the tin church next door. "Naturally I gave chase."

"And?"

"They dropped everything in their wake, so effecting their escape."

"The building was in the way for us to see this," explained one constable.

"But Christ, man, didn't you see them in the shop?"

"My back was like this to look at the people."

"Didn't they say anything?"

Kramer glared round at the crowd, which was now standing much farther back but still maintaining a lively interest. No, they wouldn't have said anything. In fact, some of the sods were smiling from ear to ear and nudging one another.

"Stuff looks like it was taken from storage," murmured Gardiner, tapping the corner of a cornflakes carton with his fingerprint case. "Maybe they stayed in the back. Let's take a look."

The minister, whose white collar and black bib were all that he was wearing under his sagging tweed jacket, made a self-important bid to accompany them, but was motioned back.

Gardiner scored half a mark. Just inside the rear door, a relatively clean rectangle in the dust on a packing case indicated where the carton had stood. The other half went to Kramer when they discovered that the till was now quite empty.

"Can you remember which divisions the coins were in?" asked Gardiner helpfully.

"Hell, no. They'd been scattered about by the first lot. Worth trying still?"

"Even though the others must have worn gloves, I don't see why not."

"Hey, just a minute—why's there no mud? Lucky's tracked it all over the place. Come, I'll show you."

Kramer led Gardiner back to the rear door and pointed out the big puddle immediately outside it, which had been caused by the constant dripping of a tap standing nearby. The storekeeper's teapot and chipped cup were inverted on a half brick beneath it.

Gardiner dusted his brush over the wooden doorstep coated in green enamel.

"Thought so," he said. "Got a sole print for you—and another. Didn't want to get their feet wet so they jumped it. I'll lift them in case they come in useful."

Of course, they had only been youngsters. Kramer felt he was beginning to lose his grip. And petty theft wasn't his job anyway. Jesus.

No, his first instinctive reaction had been right. "Ja, you do that. Could help us nail the buggers if we need them for elimination on the till. A big hope—and a lot of bloody extra work. Look, I'm just going across to see if Zondi has had any joy."

Gardiner nodded and got on with the job, suddenly absorbed in what he was doing. Should have been an artist.

Kramer was trailed across to the tin church by a raggle-taggle of big eyes and round potbellies who were hoping for a glimpse of his gun. One was rescued by its mother, who pounced with a squawk like a brown hen.

The windows were the proper pointed shape, but had been glazed with ordinary glass, some of it now broken and all of it so dusty it was difficult to see through. Kramer found a convenient hole and peered in.

Bantu Detective Seargeant Mickey Zondi was holding court, with his snap-brim hat set very straight on his head. He sat at the minister's table on the low, shaky platform, cool and dapper in his silver-thread suit despite the heat, and listened solemnly as a weeping woman, on a bench placed below him, gave her statement.

He was a terrible man for dramatic effects.

Yet Kramer could see that his improvisation was being received with due respect and, more importantly, might even be getting some real results at last. So he decided to have a smoke until there was a break in the proceedings.

Zondi stepped out of the building only a few seconds later. His eyes had always been quick.

"Well?"

"Same as before, boss. They hide when they hear the gun go off. When they look up, all they see is a red car driving away."

"Was a blue one last time."

Zondi shrugged. "The shop was empty—at least, nobody was inside when they came. They all say it was very quick."

"Uh-huh. Not just a bit frightened, you think? Don't want to get in trouble with the gang?"

"*Aikona,* these are very simple people, and the minister is a good man, much respected. You heard he chased those boys?"

"Where were you, man? Hey?"

"Busy," said Zondi, his flip manner subsiding. "Lucky's wife is very, very sad that this happened. She came in a taxi and I talked with her over the other side."

"Oh, I thought maybe she was the—"

"Boss, she says that Lucky cashed up last Friday."

"Uh-huh?"

"She is educated, so she helped him with the books. She swears to God there was at most five rand in the shop, mostly very small change because the people here have very little money anyway. Perhaps one note."

"*Five rand?* Christ, would Lucky put up a fight for that? Why the hell shoot him?"

Zondi shrugged and suggested, "To keep their faces unknown?"

"Huh! Would he have informed on them for five rand either? Never, man—that's crazy. It's crap."

They stared at each other for what seemed a very long time.

Before Kramer said, "Are we sure these *are* robberies? Not murder?"

Because ever since going into town, he had felt very strongly that somehow he had got hold of the wrong end of a stick.

3

Gardiner paid the sergeant behind the canteen bar for his two drinks and edged back through the tiny, crowded room, lethal with flying darts, to a corner table. The place was always packed, being open for only two hours from 4:30 P.M., but the booze was the cheapest in town and the company congenial. On most evenings, that was.

His companion, Klip Marais, sat hunched and glowering sourly at the wall, looking more than ever like a rough-hewn wrath of God. He had drawn in his upper lip, and was nibbling on his blond mustache, clearly not caring for the taste much.

Gardiner put down the rum and Coke at Marais's elbow and squeezed into his own seat.

"Cheers," he said, mixing his Coke with vodka.

"Huh."

"*Ach,* come on, Klip—what's got your Tampax in a twist?" Gardiner demanded.

"It's nothing," he muttered, poking at the ice in his glass. "I'm just pissed off, that's all."

"Because of what Kramer did at the Wigwam?"

"That and other things. I mean, he did put me in a bloody spot, didn't he? Left me holding the can? Chucking all those reporters out when he had no right. No crime had been committed—it was up to Monty to say whether they could be there or not. Private property. Then there was the duty officer not telling him. Oh, ja, bloody old typical Trekkersburg. . . ."

Marais was a new man. With his recent promotion, he had had to accept a transfer down from Johannesburg. After life in the metropolis, he seemed to regard a city of even 100,000 as hardly bigger than a *dorp* where not a soul dared to miss church more than once on Sundays.

33

"Lieut's got a lot on his plate," Gardiner said.

"It doesn't stay there for long! All afternoon me and Zondi have been going through the Peacevale dockets trying to find some connection between the coons that got shot."

"While . . . ?"

"He runs around as usual, like a buffalo with its bum on fire."

They had their first laugh then. Gardiner found it an apt description of Kramer's short visit to the nightclub.

"How's the guts?" he asked.

"So-so. . . . But he was pleased with the prints you got him off the inside of the till. Seems if we nail these *tsotsis,* then the other must belong to one of them."

"Zondi looking yet?"

Marais consulted his fancy navigator's watch.

"Ja, been out since four."

"The sex-mad fool," quipped Gardiner, imitating a catch phrase from *The Goon Show.*

But Marais, who did not go for this twenty-year-old BBC radio show, still popular in South Africa, gave him no encouragement.

Instead he tried some humor of his own: "I bet you'll never guess where the Big White Chief is tonight!"

Zondi parked his vehicle, then checked his PPK automatic before getting out. It was dark and he might have a long way to walk.

He cut across the open ground that served Peacevale for a football pitch and then into long grass running beside a stream. His pace slowed as he took care not to rip his shins on the rusty tins and other rubbish hidden there.

But before the moon was out, he had arrived at a dwelling no higher than his waist and constructed haphazardly out of empty cement bags wired to the tube frame off the back of some old truck. A small fire was burning in front of the entrance, heating up whatever was in the jam tins.

"Mama Thembu," he said quietly. "Where do I find your son tonight? It is a friend who asks."

A bundle of rags slithered far enough out of the interior for the flames to catch the rheumy eyes of a raddled old crone. One winked at him.

He handed over a ten-cent piece and felt the scratch of her

34

talons on his palm. Then waited patiently while she knotted the coin in the corner of a filthy head cloth.

"In Plymouth," she said, and disappeared again, like something under its rock.

Zondi was relieved. His wife, Miriam, had gone back to KwaZulu for a funeral and the children were waiting at home to be fed. He hadn't, as he had feared, far to go.

He continued along the bank of the stream until coming to an improvised bridge, where he crossed over. There were bushes, too, on the far side; thistles and stinkweed, fences that had become barbed-wire snares, and a lot of strange little noises. Rats, for the most part.

The moon—which was at only half strength—rose in time for the huddle of forgotten tin lavatories, each marked NATAL ROADS DEPARTMENT, to confirm he was on course. Way up at the top of the ridge he could see candlelight in the windows of the houses, and hear children shrieking their night games. He wondered what his own were doing.

Slipping through a gap in a wattle-plank wall, he entered the junkyard. It was really just a dump now, as nothing left in it was worth salvaging, and nobody ever went there on business—except the man he was hoping to contact. A secretive man who made secrets his business.

Zondi proceeded cautiously into a circle of old wrecks, his flashlight ready in his left hand, to leave his right free if need be. Oldsmobile, Dodge, Oldsmobile again, Studebaker, Ford, Ford, Ford . . . Plymouth.

As he advanced toward it, the driver's door creaked and swung open.

Yankee Boy Msomi, wrapped warm in his heavy overcoat with its fur-trimmed collar, sat very upright on the back seat, his smooth fingers curled over the top of his walking stick. He smelled of whiskey and had two-thirds of a bottle propped next to him on a pile of magazines. Yet his big, soft-boiled eyes, with pouches beneath them like black egg cups, focused sharply on his visitor.

"Well?" asked Zondi, sitting sideways on the driver's seat to keep his feet on the ground. "It was Lucky Siyayo's turn today. What have you heard?"

Msomi shook his head mournfully from side to side.

"Nothing? All the drinking places? You've been at every shebeen? How are they spending their money?"

35

"Today," said Msomi, "a little bird says they get just enough bread for the petrol."

It was his idea of a joke. Still, it showed how good his sources of intelligence were, and that was what mattered.

"I now have another question, Msomi: these shopkeepers —is there anything that makes them brothers?"

"We are all brothers, man."

"Something that ties them together. Get it? So these killings could be for another reason?"

Msomi blew a slow raspberry. Then got giggles, rocking back and forward until Zondi grabbed him by the hair and held it a few seconds longer than was necessary.

"Cool it, baby, cool it," protested Msomi, patting down his Afro. "No way, but *no way* is that how I read it. These guys may float like a butterfly and sting like a bee, but that's it, man. They just ain't got it together yet. Dig? This some white pig's bullshit?"

"What you say?"

"Hey, man! I asked you, I said cool it. Or you don't get no more."

"Your mother's arse!" flared Zondi in Zulu.

Msomi murmured two names.

An hour later, Zondi had both the young *tsotsis* in custody. Not progress exactly, but things were beginning to happen . . . at a price.

The *Gazette* crime reporter asked for a receipt to hand in with his expense sheet, and told the waiter to bring back two small brandies with it. Then he insisted that Kramer take a cheroot.

From the way he was carrying on, anyone would have thought they were dining at some posh place and not at Georgie the Greek's, which sold more milk shakes than hard liquor, yet the kid obviously found enough in these surroundings to support a grander fantasy. It was his trade, after all. He had actually tugged the knot in his tie down to half-mast, just as they did in the comics, and his heavy-framed spectacles rested knowingly near the tip of his button nose.

"You leave it to me, Lieut," he said in his deepest voice. "Chief sub's holding me a space on the front and tomorrow it'll be there. I appreciate you taking me into your confidence. I mean that."

36

Experience might someday teach him that people would tell him things in confidence to prevent him from publishing what he might have worked out for himself.

"Lieut?"

"Just see you keep it that way, Brian."

"Keith," said Kramer's host.

"Ja, Keith, because the message must go between the lines."

"I promise there'll not be a word of how it might spread to Trekkersburg. Make it sort of a color story. How the free-milk ladies were in Peacevale at the time Lucky Seesaw was shot, unaware of what was going on in broad daylight. They, being a charity, make it a dead cert. Maybe get a quote from one of them: 'No, I don't think we need police protection. All the Africans are so grateful to us that I'm sure we won't come to any harm.' Something like that. Y'know."

"Best you leave us right out of this."

"Anything you say."

Kramer's sigh misted the inside of his raised wineglass. This was the third time he had tried to ensure that while the city's white and Indian traders would be able to put two and two together, the gang wouldn't be presented with ideas it had not—by some small chance—had already. His theory of another motive for the deaths had been pooh-poohed by the colonel, probably quite rightly.

The receipt and brandy arrived.

"Any way of seeing your article first?" Kramer asked.

"Er—that's not usually . . . What if I read my copy over the phone to you? Give me your home number and—"

"No," said Kramer firmly. "I'll wait at the CID. That way, if it isn't right, I haven't far to come to kick your arse."

The reporter concentrated so hard on his manly laugh that he tapped his ash into the butter dish.

"Quite a day," he said after a while.

"Bloody chaos," conceded Kramer. "But I suppose this Wigwam business was a good scoop for you?"

"Ah, the general public often gets that wrong," the answer came, lightly dusted with patronage. "A scoop is something only one paper gets and no other. I could have killed Monty for that, after all the puffs I've given him."

"Hey?"

"Puffs—boosts, free publicity; not ciggies!"

He would not have been so delighted by Kramer's ignorance of newspaper slang if he had smelled hemp smoke in the misunderstanding.

"Ja, but what did Monty do?"

"Tipped off the whole of the rest of the crowd. Even the SABC was there, although they only made a par of it at the end of the regional summary. Durban evenings beat us to it, though—went like hotcakes here. Best I could manage was an exclusive—you know, an interview nobody else got, telling it in his own words. Of course, the sodding editor now says its sub judice, except for the beginning and end, because of the inquest still to come."

Kramer, who enjoyed hearing all this, grunted sympathetically.

"You should see the quotes I got! Good, hard stuff. News ed said it was a ball gripper of a story. How Monty grabbed the tart's wrists, not thinking she could be dead, not wanting to believe she was dead—as if *you* could believe that!—and then finding her arms were like 'sticks of cold wood, stiff with no hinges,' which made him realize he was too late, Jesus, and then he knew. How he'd never forget her eyes and how she looked up at him, *pleadingly,* from the other side of the grave! All that."

"What a waste."

"Don't think I didn't tear him off a bloody strip! I did. Not half. That wasn't all—I was supposed to be in chamber court at the Supreme for the divorces at eleven, and with him coming through at twenty to, I forgot to send a junior and there's been all hell about that. Garbled messages, my backside— hear he pulled one on your lot, too. That bastard has the nerve of—"

He suddenly looked like someone who just might have accidentally said the wrong thing.

As far as Kramer was concerned, he had. If it hadn't been for the abortive journey into Trekkersburg, the till would never have been tampered with.

"Who told you this? Who'd you hear it from?"

"Steady, Lieut, it's only what your sergeant explained to me after we'd been kicked out. I'm not necessarily saying Monty did anything deliberately."

"You are."

"Just an opinion, sort of slipped out. He is publicity mad,

isn't he? Who wouldn't be with a dump like that? Especially when his opposition in the lane is so good—he's imitating it with tent motifs and all."

"I don't get the connection."

"Makes a better story, that's all. You chaps coming tearing in. You should have seen them."

"*You* saw them?"

"Of course, we didn't have so far to—er—come."

The reporter smiled at his inadvertent echo of Kramer's threat. But his eyes didn't see the joke, and stayed worried like those of a gossip with no stomach for confrontation.

"Not that he was any more explicit when he rang us," he added hastily. "Didn't have to be, really, because our diary had bugger all on it worth a lead. But don't take my word on any of this—you could say I'm feeling a bit biased."

"I won't," said Kramer, throwing down enough to cover his share of the meal and a tip.

"Look, this was on me!" the reporter protested, also getting to his feet. "This was our first-ever get-together; I'll see to it, and you the next."

Kramer ignored him. He was checking to see that he had his lighter.

"Er—you won't mention I said anything, Lieutenant Kramer? And about that copy, it's early yet so it should be ready for first edition and I'll ring you as—"

"You do that, Clive," said Kramer, storming out.

Last rounds were being bought. The small black boy in bare feet, who slipped into the canteen every now and then to remove empties, his eyes never lifting above table level, was doing very well out of partly consumed soda waters and Cokes overtaken by fresh orders. If the tone of the general conversation wasn't high, its volume was, and in the hearty hubbub Marais had mellowed considerably.

"Poor bastards," he said, indicating two Portuguese guests sipping beers. "How would you like the kaffirs to kick you out of your country and have to start all over again from bottom?"

"Who brought them in?" asked Gardiner, blinking as non-smokers do in a fug. He had not lit one for three days.

"I don't know. Lots of the blokes feel sorry for them. Can't do enough for you. Want you to know how much they like it here, in the Republic, I mean. That big one's from LM, small one from Beira; got a tearoom up near the college."

"Got every bloody tearoom these days," said a young constable who overheard them. "Worse than the coolies."

Their glasses were empty.

So Gardiner led the way out, pausing to question a uniformed sergeant who was drinking an orange squash in the doorway because he was on duty, and firearms weren't allowed in the canteen anyway.

"Who's the pushy little poop, Sarge?"

"One just talking to you? Oppenheimer."

"Oh, ja," said Gardiner, and then he and Marais walked down the wide passage and out into the yard, making for the latrine. Which had batwing doors like a Wild West saloon for some amusing, if obscure, reason.

"Well, here's what I think of you," said Marais, careful to aim at Trekkersburg between the bowls because the pipes into the gutter were missing and otherwise he'd soil his moccasins. "Now for the popsie and the back row at the drive-in. Pity Mickey's made work for you or—"

The batwing doors clattered wide.

"Okay, Sergeant Marais, to my office," Kramer said softly, his hands on his hips.

Gardiner tarried to rinse out his left stocking.

Zondi handed over the keys of the Chev Commando, which was better than new now, and borrowed his bus fare off Kramer. Then he walked around Marais, gave a quick smile behind his back, and left for home.

"Look, sir," Marais began stiffly, having been given time by the interruption to prepare his defense.

"No, you look," Kramer contradicted him, and indicated he should take a seat. "I'll accept what you say about the papers in Jo'burg listening in on our radio and getting to the scene of crime just as quick. I'll accept all that."

Marais perched on the edge of Zondi's little table, relaxing slightly.

"If I hadn't been at the Wigwam, too, then it would have been a very different matter, Marais. Then I would expect you to take it personally—*very* personally. But, as it was, I had the same chances as you. The main point is this: it seems to me that there's a definite case for thinking we've been bug-

40

gered about by this arsehole who runs the club. The police, that is. I want this fully investigated. And if there is anything in it, I want charges brought against him. False information, obstruction—"

"Perjury? I've got his statement already, sir."

"Hey? First class—let me see it right now."

The prodigal left the room like there was veal on the menu, and Kramer used the delay to ring the Widow Fourie and say he would be later than planned. And yes, he had told Mickey that his help would be needed for the move to the house. He realized it could not keep being put off. He would see her.

Marais had just returned, bearing the docket, when the *Gazette* reporter rang through with his story.

"That's not bad," Kramer said, with a half smile of relief at the end of it. "Except you don't get a fusillade with five shots set days apart, hey? I do appreciate it's in English, but . . . Ja, that'll be fine. Perfect. Uh-huh, and I'll scratch yours."

He glanced across for a reaction, but Marais was too engrossed in scribbling something.

"Oh, ja? Never! 'Bye."

The receiver's weight cut the rest dead.

"I've listed them," Marais announced.

"Go ahead—read."

*"One—*suspect's report to duty officer logged at ten-thirty; for press to be there at ten-forty, calls must have been made immediately afterwards."

"Or before?"

"Hmmm. *Two*—suspect's abusive manner on finding press had been asked to wait outside."

His diplomacy was acknowledged by a curt nod.

"Three—suspect's response to learning that exhibit A was being removed from the premises. By that I mean his offer to save police time and put it in his pig bins."

"Come again?" Kramer asked, tossing over a lighted Lucky Strike.

"Ta, sir. Well, I thought Monty was just arse-creeping at the time, but obviously, now we've got this publicity angle, he hoped the snake could go in the newspaper pictures. It would have looked good, and if you can print crash pictures, I don't see why not."

"Uh-huh. Sharks—they publish killer sharks. And?"

"Four—suspect's excited manner. Warrant Gardiner was

41

telling me tonight that once Monty found a junkie dead in his bog and—"

"Hey!" interrupted Kramer. "What about number five? Now, that really interests me."

Marais had no fifth point listed. He looked up, slightly off balance.

"Sir?"

"When you're on night duty, man, what time do you get up *after* a night off? Early? Or late, like after the nights you've been on?"

"You—um—get into a sort of cycle, really. So it's usually late like the others. If you don't, by the time . . . Oh, I get you. Ten seems early for him?"

"Gives him a fifteen, sixteen-hour working day."

"Ja, but—hell, that's a nasty allegation!"

"But what?"

"According to his statement, he always comes in at ten to see the post, fix carbaret bookings, order drink and grub, and let the cleaner in."

"How do you make a reservation, then?"

"That's done through his home number—his wife sees to that. Let me see . . ."

Marais nipped a statement sheet out of the docket.

"Here it is: 'I always go into the club for a couple of hours in the morning, returning home to sleep at around noon. I had no appointments, so this was my intention until a report was made to me by Bantu Male Joseph Ngcobo, in my employ as a part-time—' "

"Never mind the pieces you wrote," said Kramer. "Just tell me where you took over."

His insight tickled Marais, who put a finger on the third line down. "From 'until a report' onwards, sir. Hell, he tried to make it a bloody book and wanted to put in hearsay."

"They all do, old son. That was a nice thought while it lasted. You were saying? Four?"

"*Ach,* just that Monty didn't seem so easily shocked before. Very cool, the warrant said. But four isn't such a big deal because, I suppose, with a female and a bloody snake like that wrapped around her neck, it must have—"

"Still there, was it?"

"Here's the photos—Kisten did a quick job."

Kramer played patience with them for a while.

"How come if she knocked its brains out on the wall it was still round her neck?"

"Doc Strydom says they've got funny nervous systems; probably locked in a spasm. You know how the wogs say that a snake can't die till sunset, doesn't matter what you do to it."

"Cut its head off with a spade and it still jumps around hours later, you mean?"

"Ja. Doc's going to check with the snake park for more details to put in the thing he's writing."

The photographs were tossed aside. They were irrelevant to the matter in hand, and Kramer was niggled at being thwarted. He had a very clear picture of the manager and an equally clear idea of what he would like. . . .

"*Six!*" he said. "What is today in Trekkersburg? And don't give me bloody Monday!"

"Wash day?" Marais postulated, with pleasing swiftness.

"Spot on. Think how the bugger was dresser. It all looked new to me. Even if it wasn't, tell me who doesn't wear his best casuals at the weekend? On Saturday arvie, or Sunday? Who goes to the trouble to posh himself up for the postman and a bloody coon boy? He didn't have any appointments. For two hours, hey? Who goes near a nightclub in the day-time? When exactly was Mr. Joseph Ngcobo admitted to the premises? With wine bottles all over the place? Dead bugs in the passage?"

Marais began to pace about, clicking his thumb against his front teeth. Then he stopped suddenly.

"What are we saying, sir?" he asked, very solemnly.

"Just this: that Monty 'Publicity Stunt' Stevenson may have reached the club before Ngcobo, checked to see if the girl had pinched anything maybe—and saw certain advantages of a commercial nature in the situation."

"Christ! You'd have to be cool to do that!"

"And what did your pal Gardiner have to say about him?" Marais slapped his thigh in self-recrimination. "But I didn't bother with times when I interviewed Ngcobo! I'm sorry, but it seemed—"

"No longer it isn't. But you got times from Stevenson?"

"Under oath."

"And Ngcobo's address? Bantu Men's Hostel?"

"That's right sir."

43

"The night is young," Kramer observed lightly.

Sergeant Kloppers and his clipboard barged into Strydom in the post-mortem room, almost dashing a jar of lungs to the floor. His night was over.

"I'm for home!" he declared defiantly.

Strydom looked round at the clock over his bifocals and frowned. "You were off most of the afternoon, so what nonsense is this? You can't expect every week to run smooth as the last. We're having a heavy run, that's all—and that's why I took the trouble of offering you a break while I was detained at Peacevale. You were gone three hours."

"Peacevale I heard about!" snapped Kloppers.

"We can't all spend our day worrying to tell you—"

Kloppers began to stab rudely at his list.

"The Peacevale coon, okay. But then? White female in a G-string. A white abortion. A—"

"Term miscarriage!" Strydom corrected, goaded into uncharacteristic pedantry.

"A whatsit. But then? A coon full of glass. And now—"

"*Ach,* for crying out loud, who said we were going to try and get through them all tonight?"

"Ah," said Kloppers, "ah, but you just come and see *what else* I find in my fridge!"

Strydom stalked through into the other room.

"That happens to be mine," he said coldly. "And I agree, you had better go home. What's more, tomorrow I'm having a word with your superiors—you're not fit for the job!"

"Suits me fine!" Kloppers shouted from the door.

And Nxumalo, who had taken the python in his stride, wondered if Sergeant Van couldn't possibly come back soon.

Gardiner laid the prisoners' sole prints and his originals on the desk in front of Kramer, who had just made a start on Stevenson's statement.

"One fits," he said, "the other doesn't. Could have been one of Lucky's biggest boys. I could—"

"Whoa, there! What's the prisoner's story?"

"Real *skelms,* those two. Saw a chance and took it. Zondi had been held up by an informer ringing, so he gave them the brush and they admitted. He's handed the case over to

44

Sithole and told him to ask for a remand to keep the thing quiet meantime."

"And the prints in the till?"

"I'm sorry, Lieutenant, but the one that *wasn't* Lucky's belongs to one of these. Him."

"And we don't keep sole prints on file."

"Some, but this other one doesn't match. We forget them?"

"Uh-huh."

"Bet you the gang will hit again tomorrow," Gardiner offered as a parting remark. "I would, if I was that good but only got myself peanuts."

It did not help to have the obvious put into words. Kramer was plunged into a bleak thought so overwhelming that he almost missed hearing what Marais returned to report.

"The cleaner Ngcobo was himself early this morning," he told Kramer. "And he went into the club actually with Stevenson *before* ten. Wine bottles are for the Indian waiters to collect when they come on. He isn't paid to clean the passage. But he did say one thing: in his belief, the boss has been bluffing all along that he didn't know Zulu, because when Ngcobo went to tell him about the sick missus, for once the boss knew straight away what he meant."

4

So Tuesday began with the prospect of a certain good and a particular evil being done in Trekkersburg.

While it also began as the day that Mickey Zondi and the lieutenant had mutually agreed to take off so that they would be free to help the Widow Fourie with her move.

No changes of plan were made, however, despite the threat of a clash of interests later, and all was to proceed as arranged.

Which meant a very early start at 2137 Kwela Village on the outskirts of the city. Or two starts, really, as Zondi rose before his family to tidy the living room. This was completed eventually with about a dozen sweeps of the broom across the rammed earth floor. Then he put six handfuls of maize porridge in a pot on the Primus stove, found the bowls, and hunted for the golden syrup. He discovered it in a tin inside another tin that had water in the bottom to keep the ants off. Miriam was a resourceful wife, as her lacy tablecloth of cleverly scissored newspaper showed. And, having domestic details now forced upon him by circumstance, Zondi also admired how she had fashioned a new handle for her flatiron from cotton reels. Miriam, who took in washing and mending, hoped one day—when the electricity was put in—to have saved enough for a steam presser.

The porridge popped and bubbled, breaking his reverie.

Zondi lowered the flame and went into the other room, clapping his hands loudly to wake the five children. He regretted this as he did so, because it would have been good to study their faces in repose. They saw little of each other.

But hungry offspring rouse quickly. The twins were up in an instant, and had not even rolled away their mattress before the others, in the big parental bed, started fighting.

"*Hau, hau, hau!* What nonsense is this?" Zondi scolded.

46

"Put on the rest of your clothes and I will feed you some breakfast. You! Not so fast"

He grabbed the cheekier twin by his ear.

"But I am dressed already!"

"Slow down."

"But I want my porridge! Last night you didn't—"

"Your porridge you will eat here."

All the children looked at him rather shocked, right down to the youngest one struggling with her hand-me-down bloomers. This feeling for propriety surprised him.

"In *here?*" queried the quieter twin, who was more like his mother.

"You are not going into the other room now I've cleaned it for when Mama comes home—none of you."

"Even to go to school, my father?"

"No. You will all go out by this window! I have seen what a mess you can make quick as quick! You see? Then I will have only one more room to clean."

"That *is* a good idea," said the eldest girl, who was now helping with the housework and hating it. "Our father is clever!"

"Lick his toes, lick his toes!" the others chorused.

"Stop the noise," Zondi boomed, "or I take off my belt!"

"Then your pants will—"

The cheekier twin took his painful ear into a corner, complaining that his homework had been too hard to understand without help.

He went unheeded. Zondi was standing very still, trying to recapture an idea which seemed like the key to the lightning robberies. It had been suggested to him only moments before —by either something said, or something done.

No good; it was gone.

Klip Marais was also up at that hour, not having been to bed. This wasn't the fault of his stomach—for he was actually in excellent health, having rushed from the dressing room merely to be sick—but because his mind kept on racing like a mad thing.

His attitude to Kramer had undergone quite a change once he had realized he was being given a chance to vindicate himself, only he was very unsure of how to go about it.

Especially as, during the small hours in the dispassionate

solitude of his single-man's quarters, he had been forced to admit the evidence was flimsy. He looked again at his list. It was a new one—he relied a lot on setting down his problems in an orderly manner. This attempt read:

1. Clothing—too good for occasion
2. Calls—too soon after CID notified
3. Character—too flustered (W/O Gardiner says)
4. Comprehesion—too quick to understand boy

Marais was also partial to alliteration, having passed his exams largely by the help of mnemonics, which only he found less difficult to memorize than the original material.

Points 1 and 2 had lost their impact; they were too much a matter of opinion, and could be simply part of the man's normal drive to boost his image and business. Point 3 was also opinion, if you set friendship aside, and different deaths affected people different ways—he had never vomited after a road accident. Point 4 was based on the word of a native, and a particularly slow-witted one at that, with a hint of the vindictive about him. And yet . . .

Marais thought a moment and added "Clock" to the others, as this was as close as he could get to "Time factor." That was the vital issue.

He had a list of times already prepared, and was mulling them over when a sleepy constable stumbled into his room without knocking to say he was wanted on the phone.

His mind raced even faster.

The subject, Kramer remembered, had first come up in a roundabout way when the Widow Fourie suddenly asked him if he knew anything about psychology. He had answered in the affirmative, explaining that psychology was a plastic duck. And when that had not been properly understood, he said that psychology was also aiming a kick at the suspect's goolies but stopping your boot a millimeter short.

It had been about the time metrication was introduced in South Africa.

She had not mentioned psychology again for about a week after that. Then he found her reading a library book about it and questioned her interest.

Without a word, she had dug into her handbag and handed

him the letter from her eldest son's headmaster. It suggested, in a very kindly way, that she should make an appointment to see the school's psychologist. Piet, it appeared from their observations, was a very unhappy boy whose work was now being affected.

The Widow Fourie had gone to the education department and seen the psychologist, only to return home with her head whirling with the names of things she had never known existed. Like displacement and Oedipus and trauma and God knows what else.

That was why she had asked Kramer what he knew, and why she had been trying to find out from library books what it was all about. He had spent the rest of the evening reading some of the books himself—even chunks of them aloud, when they revolted him, such as: "The Oedipus complex may be defined as ideas which are largely unconscious and are based on the wish to possess the opposite-sex parent and eliminate the father."

At midnight he had thrown the books aside and told her that Piet was simply a growing boy who needed the room to grow in. Living cooped up in a top-floor flat would have driven *him* mad as a kid.

She had then started an unpleasant scene in which she revealed that her relationship with Kramer had been mooted as the possible cause of Piet's trouble. And that had gone on until daybreak, when they made love twice and he said, "We'll see."

All of which was still very fresh in his mind that morning as he stood waiting impatiently on the pavement for Zondi to turn up with the hired lorry. It was to have been picked up from an Indian car dealer at eight, and with a mountain of stuff to shift, a delay wasn't funny. The two of them would be hard at it until sunset.

The time was after a quarter to nine.

Then the lorry appeared, driven at Zondi's incurably frantic pace, with four black men in overalls clinging to the back of the cabin roof. Kramer knew it would be impolitic to ask who they were.

"Right, boss—which is first?" Zondi asked, springing down from the driver's perch.

"Better make it the breakables."

"Hey! Three of you! Come on, jump!" Zondi ordered the

49

men, and then set about organizing everything.

The Widow Fourie came down to watch—she had sent the children to the park for the day. Her yellow hair was hidden by a scarf against the dust of moving, and she wore a shapeless uniform borrowed off the nanny, so there was only her face left for him to enjoy—which he did, very much, as he had never seen her so happy and excited.

"Careful, Mickey!" she cautioned with a gasp.

But Zondi, who had begun tossing up cartons of carefully packed crockery to be caught like bricks from a scaffold, just laughed politely.

"Why don't we leave him to it?" Kramer suggested, taking her arm. "Let's go over and open up."

"Well . . . ," she said, watching over her shoulder as he led her to his car.

They drove in silence all the way out to the far western side of town, passing the airfield and shooting range, and traveling into an area of gentle hills where some of the earliest settlers had built their homes. The grass was yellow, like her hair, and the dark green of the blue gum leaves and wattles came close to the uncommon color of her eyes.

He could sense she was crying quietly when they stopped.

There it was. The big house. With a veranda all the way round, and a rain-water tank at one corner to catch the flow off its low, corrugated-iron roof. And the big garden. Three acres of weeds and lawn and vegetable plots and trees with branches just right for platforms or monkey ropes. A messy, homely place. A dump.

She was now smiling as she did when he came down on her.

Kramer, who had been saving his salary over the years for the want of something better to do with it, had simply bought Blue Haze on sight and left it to her in his will. In the meantime, the Widow Fourie would continue to pay the same rent for it as the flat had cost her.

"Control to Lieutenant Kramer, Control to Kramer," the radio intruded suddenly. "Please come immediately to HQ. We repeat, please—"

He snapped it off.

Marais almost strutted as he followed Strydom out of the main building on the way to the car park.

Where they met Gardiner, who immediately asked how come both of them were looking so smug.

"Teamwork," said Strydom, with a covert wink to convey he was being generous.

"Ja, me and the doctor here have got Stevenson over a barrel. I've just put out a call for Kramer to forget his day off."

Then it had to be good.

"*Ach,* come on, you can tell uncle," coaxed Gardiner, making his brows wag.

"I didn't sleep at all well last night," Strydom said. "That sort of a day and then Kloppers having tantrums on top of it. I was being so restless my wife threw me out of bed about six and told me to doze in the study."

"Then—" Marais tried to say.

"Naturally, sleep was quite impossible by that stage, so I started to write up my notes on yesterday's little lady. I was filling in the section of external observations when something suddenly struck me."

"It'd struck me, too," Marais got in. "But I was waiting to ring at breakfast."

"Oh, were you?" Strydom murmured, not quite hiding the doubt in his voice, then continuing briskly. "I was describing how the hands were still in position towards the extremes of the reptile—and by the way, I've had it on good authority this is the only way to handle constrictors: you have to stop them getting a grip on anything with their tail, and the head end gives a nasty bite. So she was doing the right thing, only —ironically—her panic probably gave the snake the purchase it needed. If you put yourself in her position, then you can under—"

"That's all beside the point," Marais objected.

"So what, young man? Hey? Anyway, I was describing the state of the body, noting down that rigor mortis had already started to subside, when it struck me what that stupid man kept saying when we got there. Remember? How stiff she'd been to the touch? Her legs, yes, I wouldn't quarrel—"

"So the doctor phoned to see if I remembered, too, or was he imagining, and I said that's right, he had. It's even in his statement."

"Which you took?" Gardiner asked.

"Hell, you expect people to say that, and I didn't try her arms myself!" Marais dried up abruptly, having outwitted himself in his claim to have shared the discovery.

"Beside the point," Strydom said. "The fact is her arms were flaccid and I didn't have to pull to get them on her chest. So either Mr. Stevenson didn't touch her at all—or she *was* stiff when he did so."

"Meaning?"

"He told a lie under oath whichever way you take it," Marais proclaimed. "So I've got him! No problem!"

Yankee Boy Msomi made his way with grace down a path in the grass behind a short row of shops where his friend ran a record bar. He was particularly anxious not to appear in any sort of hurry.

Only seconds before he had been sunning himself in the road over on the other side, nodding at the humble greetings of passers-by and generally feeling good, when he had taken another casual look at the old red car parked outside his friend's place. It was then he noticed that its two occupants had made no move to get out. They seemed to be waiting for something.

Perhaps for the inevitable ebb in the number of people about, that short-lived phenomenon which Msomi had frequently observed happening almost anywhere during mid-morning.

That was enough for him. Discs, even for old-fashioned windups, were big money.

He found himself breathing heavily as he reached the back door of his friend's place. Although he knew nobody was following him, he slid the bolt home after slipping inside. Then he tiptoed with great caution to the doorway into the shop, and used the shoplifter mirror to see where his friend was.

Beebop was drinking a Coke and listening to the latest from the Black Mambazo. He had no customers.

Msomi checked the car. The two men were still in the front seat.

So he poked his head around and said, sweet and low, "Beebop, play this cool, brother, but just you close that door of yours, put up the sign, and come on back here a way. There's bad, bad news outside, I tell you."

When he let go something like that for free, there were few who would hesitate or argue.

Beebop, graying slightly under his very black skin, shambled over, shut the door, snibbed the lock, flipped the sign to read SORRY FOLKS, GONE GROOVIN'! and nearly ran all the way to the safety of his storeroom.

It seemed impossible, but in the short time he obscured Msomi's view of the car—which couldn't have been more than two seconds—one of its occupants had got out and disappeared.

The light was wrong for Msomi to make out the features of the man at the wheel, and the angle made it impossible to get a look at the registration plate—he had been in too much of a hurry to note it before. Might be false anyway.

"What's the jive?" Beebop whispered. "And how did you get in here, man? That kid of mine leave the door open again? Got some good stuff back here."

"Your kid, everybody's kid." Msomi grinned. "Just you shut that door, son! Oh, yeah!"

And his pointed shoes did a little shuffle.

When he looked up, there were two men in the front seat of the car again. They drove off.

And Beebop, Jr., tried the back door, finding it yanked open in his face and his hide tanned before he could yell.

Msomi waited until the boy had been set back on his feet again and handed his broom, then drifted away, saying, "My deepest and sincerest, brother, or maybe I did a good thing there."

Indeed, perhaps he had. But in the shop next door, a butcher bled to death. They had used a .22 this time, which the high-wattage output of Beebop's speakers had simply swallowed up.

Kramer tried to make a joke of it.

"You can see they're running short," he said. "That's a lot cheaper than firing thirty-eights."

The idea wasn't to make Colonel Hans Muller laugh, just to get him to say something.

The colonel went on twisting his plastic ruler in his oddly neat hands, which would have looked like a pianist's if it hadn't been for their werewolf trimmings. His pink-cheeked big head had gone blotchy.

"They're truly making monkeys of us," he said at last, "and I don't like it. I don't like persons getting shot in my dis-

53

trict. I don't like what we both—but, man, what can we do? We haven't the availability to cover Peacevale, and who says it will be there next time?"

"Uh-huh, especially as they've gone and done it again," Kramer agreed. "Coons are lucky if they eat meat once a week, then they buy it on a Friday when their money's paid. Through the week, all the butchers keep is maybe sausages, some chicken they've cooked up themselves, offal. Their tills are nearly empty."

"And you say on one side was a record shop?"

"Sells transistors, battery players, all kinds. Number one in the district; the fat cats come in from every direction. But it was shut at the time for stocktaking."

The colonel dropped his ruler and reached for his paper knife to play with. It still had its exhibit label from a murder case.

"Okay—exactly how much this time?"

"Approximation: fifteen rand."

"Hell. Is Zondi working on this?"

"His day off, sir."

"At a time like this?"

"His wife's away and—"

"Since when has a kaff—"

This aborted beginning to what might have been quite a speech amused Kramer. The colonel had very nearly said "kaffir," which was now an officially banned word. Only the day before a traffic officer had made a public apology for saying it to one of his Bantu subordinates.

"What's so funny now?" asked the colonel. "You've got another joke to make?"

"I was just going to say he has been helping me at home with some heavy work."

"*Ach,* that's okay, then. As long as he respects you. But bring him in and see if any of his customers knows anything about today."

"And me?"

"Don't look to me for orders, Kramer! Go on, man, *voetsak!*"

Which summed up what Kramer found best in the man. He would have walked away very happily, if it had not been for the weight of trust this also placed upon him.

* * *

Zondi returned the lorry to the Indian car dealer and transferred the four black men back into his police vehicle. Then he paid them each the two rand he had told the lieutenant was the going rate for express furniture removers.

This done, he drove round the corner and onto the building site.

The white foreman, stiff-jointed from sitting on piles of bricks all day, came across to him.

Zondi showed his identity card again.

"Oh, ja, and what have these *skelms* been up to, hey? Are you going to take them all away? That's no worry."

"*Hau,* no, master! These are very good boys, master. You must trust them! They give us help too too much."

"Never."

"Most difficult case, master, but their eyes are witnessing all known facts. If you do not believe me, then you must tring-a-ling Lieutenant Kramer. *Hau,* this one tells us where the *skabenga* puts the knife in his wife's seating arrangements, and this man here—"

"Work to be done," the foreman said, turning away. "Come on, you good-for-nothing *ntombi* shaggers, get up those ladders, *checha wena!*"

Zondi, who knew he had been dismissed, from the mind as well as the vicinity, picked his way back to the car, calculating the best way to make the U-turn.

"And now, Mickey," he said in his best English to the rearview mirror, "let us adjourn for lunch."

His car had no radio, nor had Blue Haze a telephone.

The atmosphere in the post-mortem room could have been cut with a knife.

Then it became apparent that the debate had put a stop to the actual work in progress, and so Kloppers retired to sulk in his office. Leaving an aggrieved Marais facing an agitated Kramer over the legs of the dead snake dancer, while Strydom mumbled to himself as he laid down the scalp saw at the other end.

"Look, Doc, all I want to do is get this straight," Kramer said. "I'm too bloody busy to waste time on a poop. But if you're sure, then we'll have him in and get it over with."

"But, Lieutenant, sir—"

"I've heard you, Marais; now I want the expert's view."

"Then I quote to you Professor K. Simpson, pathologist to the Queen of England: 'It is unfortunate, but rigor is uncertain in its timing.' All right?"

"So it's only on average that it sets in after six hours and lasts thirty-six? She was allegedly found after thirty-four, remember, not forty-two."

"It can begin immediately. And the circumstances were exactly right for that—violent exertion prior to death, a warm room. I'd say it must have done, as it goes away again in the order it comes—head, arms, trunk, then the legs. Her legs were stiff."

"So you can be certain Stevenson didn't just break the tension by trying to lift her?"

"I see your point—stretching muscle does destroy its rigidity, Tromp—but I was obviously paying particular attention to the head, and I know it had already passed away there. And I also know it had reached the torso. The arms had to be included in that sweep; they could not have been stiff when he says they were."

"Just had to be sure," Kramer said, starting for the door. "And thanks, Doc. Coming, Marais?"

"Hell, I'm sorry, Lieutenant. I was transferred from Housebreaking down here. I didn't know all that about breaking tensions. I've always thought a stiff was just a stiff."

"Most people do," Kramer replied, his spirits restored. "But you just watch it, or you'll be landing yourself in trouble with a smart lawyer one of these days."

And they went to find Monty.

When Zondi had finally managed to arrange the living room as the Widow Mourie wanted it, she went out with him onto the stoep.

"What do you think of it?" she asked.

"*Hau,* it is beautiful," he said. "The madam's children will be very happy here. You can even buy them a donkey perhaps."

"That is an idea!"

He picked up his jacket.

"Yes, I'll ask Trompie—or do you know about donkeys?" she asked.

"No, madam, nothing." He lied without malice. As a herdboy, he had seen all he wanted of donkeys before he was seven.

"I thought all ..."

She let that tail away as her eye was caught by a white butterfly dipping by.

"I'm so happy," she said. "Does it show?"

Zondi felt embarrassed and looked around for his hat. It had been dropped in the tea chest with the lampshades.

"Are you going?" she asked.

"Is there something ... ?"

"Oh, no, Mickey, you've been a marvelous help. Just I feel lonely all of a sudden. It's so private here, isn't it? When is the lieutenant getting back?"

"That I don't know, madam. Shame."

"Of course—who ever knows that?"

She walked to the edge of the veranda and shaded her eyes to look into the trees. Grasshoppers were doing their erratic dance in the slanted rays between the trunks.

"Could I—could I possibly ask you one more favor? To fetch the kids from the park now for me, instead of the nanny sending them in a taxi at four? It's really your fault I'm at such a loose end!"

"Victoria Park? With the swings? I'll go straight away now."

"Hey, you know what? You must bring your kids here to play in July when we're at the beach. Do you think they'd like that?"

He knew they would. But that he would never have enough explanations for them afterward.

"Maybe, maybe." He laughed. "I'll go now. See you by and by."

"Oh, where are the presents for Miriam?"

"In the boot, madam—thank you, madam. *Sala gahle.*"

He drove off, thankful to escape a woman who asked so many questions, many of which left him looking tongue-tied. But he was indebted to the Widow Fourie for all the unwanted household effects, including an iron that had lost its cord, and for the children's clothing she decided to get rid of as well. She knew how to give so it didn't hurt to take from her. She seemed to do it without thinking. As she had dumped, without thinking, that very serviceable old paraffin

57

heater, which was only a little rusty, on her new rubbish heap. He had not thought it wrong to stow that in the trunk also.

A day that began like this could only get better.

5

Stevenson had to be in. A station wagon stood in the drive, and the curtains of the bay window round the side were closed. Yet Kramer looked disappointed.

"Not the smart place I thought it would be," he said, in no hurry to get out.

The Chev Commando was parked under a flame tree on the opposite side of the street.

"Well, like I say, he's up against something with the other club," Marais explained. "Got style and class."

Kramer, who had entered it on one occasion, in the hope of buying cigarettes after midnight, made a face. If a black ceiling and black walls and a black stage were considered stylish, so be it. And if Trekkersburg's high society was class, he was no one to argue. But his own response to both had been one of acute depression, so instantaneous that he had gone a mile to get his Lucky Strikes off an obliging refugee near the station. Those buggers worked all hours under very bright lights.

"Do we?" Marais ventured.

"Uh-huh. Let's go and drag him out," Kramer said, turning off the engine. "This is only one of three places I'm supposed to be."

As they went up the flagstones to the front door, past an old gymkhana poster on the gate, he wondered how things were progressing in Peacevale. His senior sergeant was in charge there, but he wished Ludwig hadn't sodded off on leave, because that was his territory. Same as Lawrence of Arabia, without the camels.

He was still not concentrating when the door opened to Marais's knock and a black housemaid peered round it. It would have seemed more natural to see the Widow Fourie.

"Yer-ba-bawl" the maid exclaimed in fright, at once rec-

59

ognizing them for what they represented, probably from their haircuts.

"Is your master in?" Marais asked. "You fetch him for us, *che-che*."

"Gladys? What are you up to? Oh, I see—you Mormons have been here pestering before!"

"Never," said Kramer, tugging Marais into the hall behind him and closing the door.

"Police, CID," the youngster got in hurriedly.

"But what is this about?"

Kramer did the stare that implied heavily his dislike of rhetoric.

She was man enough to stare right back. Her hair color was amazing—perhaps a poodle parlor did it.

Then the crimson lipstick—which claimed more lip than she owned—twisted into a mean streak.

"You must be the uncouth one," she said. "I'm sorry, but my husband's sleeping. He does conduct his affairs at night, you know."

"Uh-huh?"

"And he has taken two tablets today because one hasn't been enough lately."

"Since when? Sunday?"

That pitted her poise. She moved back a little and folded her arms.

"*Am* I entitled to know what this is about?"

"You'd better ask hubby," said Kramer. "He's the man with all the answers."

The children attended the first shift at Kwela Village School and so returned home while Miriam was still trying to find enough space to put everything and to complete her account of the funeral. They were given their new clothes to try on, and told to stay in the other room. It was raining.

"Yes, very sad," Zondi agreed, "but it will mean a little more money for us."

Like most workingmen, he did his best to help others in the family who couldn't get passes to leave the homeland and find employment.

"There, you see? You are not listening me properly. Now that there is room for another at the kraal, the aunt of my

60

sister's brother's wife will be coming to live there. Her sons all died in that mine accident."

"Were they bastards?"

"Her husband has TB. They've locked him up with the lepers in the Transkei."

"I forgot. Hey, you know? Now Lucky is dead—shot down."

"No!"

"The lieutenant is very angry with them. It was the same ones as before."

"Hau! They were stupid to shoot Lucky!"

"That's why I must go now," said Zondi, slipping on the harness of his shoulder holster. "There is a man I must see. Is this all right with you?"

Miriam nodded, holding a wasp-waist corset against the light and wondering at its potential.

"You go, you go—since when does the man ask? And I need you out of the way; this house is so dirty I must do a big clean."

Zondi left in just the right frame of mind to jolt Yankee Boy Msomi out of his lethargy.

After taking coffee with Mrs. Stevenson, Kramer knew they had a possible ally. She did not like Monty much more than they did. She almost implied the existence of their child was evidence enough to support a charge of indecent assault.

How such partnerships began Kramer would never know, but this one seemed very near its end.

"I met an American airman in England during the war," she said, "and he used to talk about 'slarbs.' That's what he is —a slob."

"Mind if I take more sugar?" asked Marais, having trouble with his cup.

"Help yourself, dear. I'll just pop out again and see if I can get him up."

Marais went purple as Kramer made a shocked grimace behind her back.

"Jesus, have a heart, sir!" He winced.

"Notice?" said Kramer. "She smells something—and she's liking it. But she told us the story about Monday morning and everything as if she'd read about it in the papers. I don't think she knows even as much as we do. If she hasn't fetched him,

61

then we'll check out his movements on Sunday with her—okay?"

Marais raised a thumb.

Mrs. Stevenson came back in and half filled the settee.

"Not as much as a moan," she said. "Oh, yes, slobs. That slob in there must have done what he did on Sunday."

"Oh, ja?"

"Took four of his blinking tablets and decided not to get up at all."

"What?"

"It's the truth. On Sunday, he came in after checking our sweet machine near the bus depot—we've got the concession, and if you don't keep emptying it the vandals try their luck—and, calm as you please, went out like a light. Must have been about one. Twelve hours later, he's still like that. And I've had a proper Sunday dinner cooked and everything. No good trying to wake him. He's still in his pit at six and—would you believe it—he didn't get up at *all* until Monday, when his lordship managed his usual time."

Her indignation was quite real.

Marais put his cup down and reached for a list.

"Twenty minutes from town to here in traffic," Kramer said impatiently.

Mrs. Stevenson was waving to someone through the window.

"Oh, look," she said. "There's Bess outside and I want a word with her about taking Jeremy to riding lessons. Are you . . .?

"I'd appreciate if we could use your phone for a moment," Kramer said, courteously rising with her. "Then maybe we best be going."

"It's in the hall, Mr. Kramer. Well, toodle-oo, if I don't see you again."

She rushed out through the French windows, making hi-there noises.

"Sir, this means his only chance of feeling the deceased was stiff—or even knowing about it—was between when she left the stage and when the snake got her or a few minutes afterwards. She couldn't have been cold either—and that's something else in his sworn statement."

"Do I look like your grandmother?" asked Kramer. "You sit tight while I ring the Chocolate Fairy."

The python was going off. Perhaps, without the bulk of a human body, a few minutes out of the fridge was enough for the putrefactive processes to continue. Snakes were strange things at the best of times, and certainly had a metabolism all their own.

This distressed Strydom under the circumstances: the largest glass bottle he had been able to find was not big enough to contain it.

Nxumalo, who was standing ready to pour in the formalin to preserve it, clucked his tongue sympathetically.

"Why doesn't the doctor-boss just skin it?" he suggested.

"Because the boss wants a better permanent record of it than that," Strydom explained. "You see, I'm hoping to deliver a paper about this case at our annual conference in Cape Town, and it would be so much more effective if a three-dimensional concept could be arranged. Understand?"

Nxumalo nodded. The boss did not want to skin it.

"Well, perhaps the museum will lend me one of their bottles," Strydom said. "I never thought of that."

"Very clever, my boss."

"Or at least they'll tell me where they got theirs from. And I want their views on its strength."

"Yes, boss."

"Pop it away for me again, then, but be extremely careful like before," Strydom ordered, and then went into the office.

Kloppers was away at lunch.

The reptile man at the museum was very quiet-spoken but showed a practical interest in the problem. He said there were no spare bottles, as that method of preservation had been abandoned years ago, and any specimens outstanding were therefore kept in a deep-freeze. However, if the district surgeon would care to drop in that afternoon, bringing his snake with him, he was sure something could be done. A break in routine would be most welcome.

Kramer replaced the receiver very quietly and stood gazing down the passage. A pair of polished black shoes waited outside the third door down.

"Okay, man, let's go," he called to Marais, adding in a whisper when the sergeant reached him, "We're not really going, hey?"

Then Kramer opened the front door, counted three, stepped back inside, and closed it.

They waited. Not a murmur.

"We try Plan B," he said into Marais's ear, knowing he would like it put that way.

Kramer took hold of a carpet sweeper, which the maid had left handy to clear away their crumbs, and wheeled it down the passage. It made very good squeaks when scrubbed back and forward. He began to bump its rubber trim against the wainscoting, and to hum one of the Zulu love chants he had heard Zondi hum so often at the steering wheel. The sweeper collided with the shoes and Kramer paused, keeping the sound in the back of his throat as high-pitched as possible.

"Oi! Gladys!" roared a wide-awake voice behind the door. "Bloody bitch, think you're back in your kraal, do—"

"Hello again," said Kramer as the door was jerked open.

"You!"

"And you. Come in the front room for a moment—don't bother to change."

Years of calling on homes early in the morning had taught Kramer that unless a man went in for boxing or wrestling, he generally felt most vulnerable in his dressing gown. And it certainly saved everyone time.

Presently, seated in a black silk kimono, with Japanese egg stains, Monty Stevenson told them everything he knew. It was the same old story, with the alibi of the sweet machine tacked on the end.

"Have to have a finger in a lot of pies in my game," he explained. "There's the club and my traveling disco for house parties, then my catering course for Indians, and I'm negotiating rights for—"

"Uh-huh. But according to a bus inspector I know, your chocolate machine at the depot is empty."

"Wonderful news—knew it would catch on."

"Because it's broken."

"What?"

"Smashed by vandals on Saturday."

"The bastards!"

"All bluff," Kramer admitted, adding for Marais's benefit, "Remember, that bus inspector needs a kick up the arse sometime—said he'd got better things to do than doing stupid inquiries for CID."

"Then it's not bro—"

And that was it. The quick flip-flop of conflicting fact caught up with Monty Stevenson and laid him low. Then he told them the true story of what had happened at the Wigwam that weekend.

He'd met this very old friend and they'd taken a bottle of the best into his office to enjoy it in private and then he'd suddenly noticed the time and had to rush home and lie because she didn't like this particular old friend very much. Who had, unfortunately, left town for a job opportunity in Australia.

"That's what I wanted to hear," said Kramer.

"Thank God."

"So get dressed. You're under arrest."

There was an obvious place to look. For all his healthy cynicism, Yankee Boy Msomi was a hypochondriac. And the private surgery of Dr. Arthur Pentecost Thlengwa, which took in hundreds of rand a day, welcomed his drop in the ocean. It was Msomi's kidneys that primarily concerned him.

But he was not in the long queue of people who preferred to pay for their suffering.

So Zondi half-heartedly tried the pandemonium of the overcrowded outpatients at Peacevale Hospital, and drew another blank.

He was third-time lucky back in the lower end of Trekkersburg, where the herbalists and witch doctors had their shops in a modern block with prosperous Indian families living above them. Msomi was studying a rack of desiccated baboons and other specialist items outside the entrance to Ntagati and Son. He had already made several purchases, which stuck out of his overcoat pocket.

Zondi parked on the other side of the street and was quickly camouflaged by idlers too idle to notice who he was, and who chose his car to lean against.

The problem was making discreet contact with Msomi in daylight. But now that he knew where Msomi was, he knew he could always follow him until the right moment came. One thing was for sure: Zondi was not going to be given the slip.

He began the wait by lighting a cigarette.

Msomi must have seen something in the reflection of the shopwindow, because he turned and, to Zondi's great surprise, gave him the nod.

"Sta-tion," he mouthed, and then went back into the store. To anyone else watching it, it would have looked like nothing more than a man fighting off a sneeze.

They met on platform 2 behind a pile of mailbags, screened by rough rustics wearing blankets and sitting on wooden suitcases.

"Where are you going?" Zondi demanded.

"To the tribal homelands, you dig? Way, way away. Things is hottin' up here and it's time I went see where my roots come from."

Then he told Zondi hastily about what had occurred in Beebop's shop, and about the slaughtered butcher, who was a stranger to them both. And rounded off by agreeing that the robberies were something else.

"Brother, it's this way. A guy here, a guy there, they know how I make a bit of bread on the side, see? Now just say I do pick up somethin' that spins you by the tail—what then? What if I don't, but word gets out anyway? And they think it's me? Can I convince them? Let's say the big heat is really on and—"

"They kill you to shut you up?"

"There you have it, little bird. Yeah, man. But if I'm outa town when it happens—well, groovy, baby."

"You've hung six hard men on the rope," Zondi reminded him. "What scares you so much this time?"

"What I've done seen today with my own two eyes! Guys comin' and goin' and nothin' in between."

"Huh!"

Zondi thought it over. Msomi had a ticket and a bag which must have been standing in Ntagati's. He plainly meant to be on that train north. Therefore he had arranged this meeting because he knew that Zondi would follow him and he wanted his departure to be unimpeded by misunderstanding. That all made sense. But not his degree of apprehension.

"*Aikona*, those two eyes saw more," said Zondi. "You've got papers to travel?"

"Cool it, Mickey. Since when did Yankee—"

"Sergeant! Sergeant to you And it'll be a sergeant who arrests you, here right now, if you don't speak the rest!"

There was a great hiss of steam and the enormous locomotive, pushing its water tender, slid in on platform 2, bringing the rustics to their feet. It was Msomi's train, too.

Zondi caught him by the hair on his coat.

"Okay, okay," Msomi said despairingly.

"Then what?"

"Chainpuller! Now can I blow?"

Zondi let go. Watching Msomi run for a place on the benches, and feeling a clawed fist grab the walls of his stomach.

Chainpuller.

The walls were pale lime with scuff marks. A map of Trekkersburg almost covered one of them. There was a gray filing cabinet to which a calendar had once been glued. A small table with a stool, and a large desk with pigeonholes and a chair. Two wire wastepaper baskets and a pair of telephones. Two ashtrays: one an inverted piston head, the other an empty paper-clip tin. A wooden pole with a leather loop at one end. Daubs of white paint saying CID on anything worth stealing. In other words, the office was not much to look at, but it had atmosphere.

Monty Stevenson apparently thought so. He stood on the scarred linoleum flooring as if expecting matter-of-fact violence to be done to his person at any moment. He shivered.

And the walls went on whispering.

"Still here?" inquired Kramer, just back from the same old story in Peacevale, yet with calculated suddenness behind his back.

Stevenson went rigid, which had its comic side.

Kramer picked up the pole, slipped the thong over his wrist, and let it swing to and fro.

"Getting stuffy," he remarked, and used the pole to open both fanlights. Then he hung it up on its hook.

Marais came in, dusting the sugar from his teatime doughnut off his chin, and burping with selfish satisfaction. He picked up his notebook.

"Where had you got to?" Kramer asked. "How many more stories is he going to tell?"

"Swears it's the truth now, sir."

"Uh-huh."

"But it *is!* I'm prepared to—"

"You shut up."

"Can't I even sit down, please?"

"Seen Zondi?" asked Kramer, seating himself at his desk. Marais was already back on the stool.

"Er—no, sir. Well, now it goes like this. After seeing the last customer out of his club at twelve-twenty on the night in question, he then—"

"Got his name?"

"It was one of my members, so I've—"

"Carry on, Marais; the time was twelve-twenty."

"He went to close his office, remembering there he had business matters to discuss with Miss Bergstroom, the dancer. It was her last night of the booking and he would not be seeing her again. So he went to the dressing room and found she had been, quote, the victim of a tragic mishap, unquote. The snake was still moving slightly, but he could see it, too, was dead. His first reaction was to ring for the ambulance—and us —then he admits realizing the situation could, as you suggested, be turned to his advantage. He knew that by then the Sunday papers were already being printed and that on a Saturday night the daily papers usually had only a junior poopsqueak on call. By the way, the prisoner once worked on the advertising part of a paper, so that's how he knows all this."

"Births or deaths?" asked Kramer.

"So the point is, sir, he knew that raising the alarm then wouldn't bring him the kind of attention he wanted, but he denies that he arranged matters so the press would be there before we. In all other aspects, it's much the same as we worked out together. He's prepared to give another full statement, although I have informed him of his rights."

"Yes, Officer. I thought that if I left everything just as it was, and had the boy go in there on Monday, then I wasn't really doing any wrong. I mean, what harm could possibly come of it?"

"Now you know," said Kramer.

Marais, the clown, wrote that down.

"By the way, Stevenson, did Miss Bergstroom have an agent?" Kramer continued after a pause.

"Of course! I don't hire any old act for—"

"Then how come you had to talk business with her?"

"I'm sorry? What was that?"

Kramer laughed and stretched, lifting an imaginary pair of barbells, and arching his back.

"I look at it this way, Stevenson," he said. "I know a bit

about papers, too, you see. A morning one like the *Gazette* or the *Durban Herald* has a hell of a hard time filling its front page on a Monday with only the weekend to pick from. Man, the times I've been in a charge office on a Sunday morning and the reporters have practically begged me to take my gun and make some news. I agree with you about the early hours, but that doesn't apply to around eleven—then you can't hope to get better service. Everybody gets so sick of car crashes and sailing regattas and all that rubbish, and they miss the good juicy court stories. You could have gone in on Sunday, hey? Why not?"

Stevenson began to tremble properly.

"Ja, I thought so," said Kramer. "If you'd said you'd just popped along to see how Miss Bergstroom was doing, your wife would have been suspicious, hey? And with good reason? Even so, you could have invented some excuse if you weren't all tangled up by your guilty secret."

"Hey?" said Marais.

"The actual reason Mr. Stevenson wanted to see Miss Sexy Snake Seventy-*voetsak*—and the actual nature of the business. Am I right?"

The prisoner sat down just where he was on the floor.

Marais looked almost sorry for him.

But Kramer had just had another thought, and picked up the statement made by the cleaner. There was still the matter of the rigor mortis to tidy up.

"According to the boy Joseph, you dismissed him before entering the dressing room a second time. Did you in fact enter it?"

Stevenson took all the breath he could hold and said, "Only for a moment. I couldn't stomach the smell then—nor the sight. It haunted me all Sunday in nightmares, quite different if you—I mean, I'd had too long to think about it. And that's the honest reason why I was turned up when I telephoned and—"

"If you want to know, that was your big mistake."

"Saying she was stiff," added Marais.

"But she was dead and don't all . . .?"

"*Ach,* these laymen," sighed Marais, getting him to his feet.

"So you never even touched her the first time," Kramer

said, finding that a more interesting comment.

"I—I could see all I wanted to. Her breasts weren't moving—and she did look stiff! Like sticks, those arms were."

"And how did you know her heart had stopped? Or would you get lipstick on you doing the kiss of life?"

"*What?* Oh, dear God, is that what all this has been about? You mean she might still have been alive? Like a drowned person? That I could have—y'know?"

Kramer, who had only just had the idea, shrugged.

"The post-mortem report will be here in a few minutes if you'd like to wait," he said matter-of-factly.

Emmerentia, who was Strydom's lovely and gifted small granddaughter, called Trekkersburg Natural History Museum the "dead zoo."

He was thinking of this with a fond smile as he walked up the steps into its entrance hall and stopped at the reptile cases, which were new.

And yet, Strydom discovered, not everything in this section was as dead as it looked. By waiting patiently, and watching for a flicker of tongue, it was possible to distinguish between exhibits that were inanimate and those that were lifeless, so to speak.

The excellence of the preserved specimens was such that he was sure he had come to the right place. In fact, he would have returned for a second look, had not a Zulu attendant— with immense wooden plugs in his earlobes—pounced suddenly to polish his breath marks from the glass.

Strydom continued down a short passage and into the large mammals hall. It was huge and vaulted, with a gallery for insects and anthropology, and echoed so readily that he went up on tiptoe to skirt a charging bull elephant. A pair of giggling children—which reminded him it was the Michaelmas holidays—were comparing the back ends of the black and the white rhino.

And there were more children, only Bantu this time, and in their best bib and tucker, in a solemn line outside the door he had been told to make for. There a harassed museum official was trying to explain something to the black teacher in charge. Strydom hoped it would not take all day.

"Then if you only read the poster about the wildlife film

show for the kiddies from a bus, you can hardly blame us for the disappointment," the official was saying. "There's plenty else to look at."

" 'For Whites Only' was in very small writing," the teacher replied, showing not anger but a certain stubbornness. "To tell you the truth, when I brought my pupils in just now, I again failed to notice the restriction concerning the film theater."

"Well, I'm glad you're prepared to tell the truth!" said the official, trying to laugh it off.

"I simply thought, sir, as the theater is not even a quarter occupied, that under the circumstances we may be allowed to stand at the back."

"Not my ruling. Sorry. Don't make the rules. And I've got a boss waiting, so that's the end of it."

The teacher turned away and told the children it was time to go and buy their cold drinks. He would pay.

"I'm Smith," the official said, shaking Strydom's free hand. "I was sent down to meet you and—oh, never mind. It's this way. That's quite a size. Bose as in rose."

Smith opened a door for Strydom at the top of three flights of stairs and excused himself.

The room had a very high ceiling and enormous windows which filled it with the cold light of the rain clouds. The furnishings were awesomely Victorian, and Strydom felt as thought he had stepped back through time to his medical school. Some of the smells were familiar, too.

"Good afternoon. I'm Strydom, the DS," he said to a large man with white hair working at a table. "You're Mr. Bose?"

The expert turned round and stared vaguely, as if he wasn't prepared to say anything until this vision had fully materialized. Then his manner changed.

"The python?" he asked softly.

"That's right. Here—you take it and tell me what you can do for me, what the chances are."

Strydom drifted over to the table and saw that Bose had been engaged in painting a perfect plaster cast of a puff adder, applying his colors a scale at a time. So that was how it was done.

"Not what I expected," said Bose.

Strydom looked round. The python had been laid out

along the edge of a bench and Bose was gently feeling its middle.

"Well, I did describe the circumstances."

"That's just it. Or did you break its back?"

6

When the full post-mortem report on Sonja Bergstroom arrived by messenger from the district surgeon's office, Kramer took Marais aside and handed him a page.

"What's all that boil down to?" he asked.

Marais read carefully and then said, "Instantaneous?"

"Uh-huh, near enough. But there's no need to go shouting about it."

"Why? Don't you think he's telling the whole truth yet, sir?"

"Man, I'm not sure. It sounds okay—but I think you should first worry him a bit more. You never know. Here—look at this."

And he handed Marais another page.

"Hell, a semen stain!"

"External. No sign of sexual interference or recent intercourse, Doc notes. He's just put it down for the record, query analysis. Could be older than Saturday night and we don't know the young woman's bathing habits. With her kind, that's show business, Marais."

"But it'll give us a group?"

"Uh-huh."

"And if it's the same as . . ."

"Not much relevance in court, but the idea will fry the bastard nicely all the same. She took a break between acts—get what I mean?"

Marais got. He reddened, being young for his age.

"But how do we . . . ?"

"I'll think of something," said Kramer, beginning to stroll back to his office. "She had a divan in there, right? And an ashtray? Waste bin? What kind does he smoke?"

"Small cheroots. But with all due respect, sir, I mean—is this really necess—er?"

73

"Ask her next of kin when you see them again, old son. That's who I work for."

She had none, but Marais seemed to get the point all the better for that.

Zondi tried three informants, and lost each in a cloud of dust at the mention of Chainpuller Mabatso. As the lieutenant said on these occasions, it was like trying to interest virgins in a rape course. Whatever that meant exactly.

But as far as Chainpuller himself was concerned, Zondi now felt there was little doubt involved.

The how and why were another matter.

Chainpuller put a shudder through most men. Not because he was big—he was five foot one; or because he was enormously strong—he used two hands to shell a peanut. But because he was tangibly evil.

Whereas Zondi would throw himself on a man half again as big as himself, prepared to gouge and bite and take as much in return, the thought of touching Chainpuller lightly with one finger was more than he considered the call of duty. It was like being expected to handle one of those flat scorpions, the dull gray kind that skitter in the corner of rooms where dead tramps are found, somehow very wise and aware of your fear of them.

There was more to Mabatso than that. After his ten years in a penal colony, to which he had been sent, as a robust youth, on the word of his brother, Chainpuller had created for himself a reputation for obsessive privacy. Even the brother had moved away from their hut—nobody was ever sure where to.

While Chainpuller lived on alone, high on a slope overlooking Peacevale, sitting with his back against the porch upright and watching. Ostensibly he had become a witch doctor, and wore inflated pig bladders in his plaited spikes of hair, but as no one seemed ever to visit him, at least during daylight hours, word got around that he was really a wizard.

Word also got around—more times than Zondi could remember—that whenever there was a mysterious death in the township, Chainpuller was behind it. The wizard did nothing to discourage these rumors, and when challenged by a relative made reckless through grief, would simply make a fresh mark in the mud wall beside him.

74

Yet no police investigation had ever been able to link him in any other way to what had happened.

Once, another black sergeant had tried to prove that the gifts of cash left near the hut were not given in charity but as blood money—payments made to have the donor relieved of a burdensome wife or mother-in-law. This sergeant had died in his sleep before bringing any charges.

Such stories made the lieutenant laugh, and call Zondi a superstititious kaffir, yet even he stood back when a visit to the hut was demanded of them. Just as the arrival of certain people can make you suddenly in a party mood, in the same way Chainpuller's presence was like having shadow put in your blood.

So a common denominator between Chainpuller and the robberies could be found in the uncanny. This was, however, at the level of pure gossip and rumor, and Yankee Boy Msomi operated some way above that.

Making the idea at once less acceptable and twice as much worth looking into.

Zondi's wait was rewarded. He snatched the passer-by from the street and handcuffed him to a drainpipe.

"I will leave you there for Chainpuller," he snapped, "unless you and me have a good talk together."

This one was not going to get away.

Kramer splashed up through the puddles to the door of the Wigwam and found Joseph Ngcobo hunched there on his haunches, using the drizzle to soften his half loaf of stale bread.

"Come to clean, hey?"

Ngcobo sprang up beaming, quickly swallowing his last mouthful, showing all the painful eagerness of a poor man paid by the day. Then his face fell.

"Boss not coming this morning," Kramer explained, flipping him a coin for his trouble, glad that Zondi wasn't there to make him feel a fool.

"*Hau*, thanks!" said Ngcobo, getting the hell out before lightning hit him next.

Untrue. The boss was coming. It was just that Marais had been unable to find a parking place, and the now pathetically cooperative Stevenson had offered up his personal bay in a multistory one short block away.

Kramer tried the Yale key, stepped inside, and left the door unlatched. Then he saw a new show card propped on a child's easel that had been covered in glitter. The card announced: YOU KNEW HER—YOU LOVED HER—SEE THE ROOM WHERE IT HAPPENED—MEMBERS ONLY—NOTHING HAS BEEN TOUCHED!

It made him proud to be a pig.

A note had been left in the eagle's beak in the phony totem pole disguising a coat stand. The message was that someone signing himself Mohammed had finished work at 4 A.M. and respectfully requested prompt payment—in cash—of the sum agreed.

That sent Kramer clattering down the steps and across the stage. The warning notice had gone and the passage was carpeted in blue and had striped wallpaper over the cracks. Even the little stairs had been covered.

He took them at a bound, examined the key ring, chose a chunky old-fashioned one, and hurried down the passage.

There was no keyhole in the door with the star on it. Just a bolt on the inside.

His fist smashed into the paneling.

"Marais!" he bellowed.

"Coming, sir! Stevenson was just worrying the painters hadn't closed the front door behind them properly and—"

"Marais! Look at this, man! And tell me what sort of person—especially if she's just driven a lot of sex maniacs half mad—walks around, bare-arsed, in her room without locking the door first? *Hey?*"

"Oh, Eve wouldn't have done that," Stevenson agreed obsequiously. "She hated strangers bothering her—and the snake was loose, too, and he was terribly expensive. What if he had escaped into the club and one of my members took a—"

"Shut up! Ja, Marais?"

"I don't know, sir."

"And you, Stevenson?"

"Well—um—didn't think of it at the time. So much else on the go."

"That seems to be the trouble with quite a lot of people around here."

Marais went into the dressing room and came out again.

"Sir, it's possible that in her struggle she tried to get out and get help and had pulled the bolt back before—"

"And which hand did she use?"

"That's when the snake got the better of her!" said Stevenson. "She had her hand off and—"

"Which hand?" Kramer repeated. "She'd never let go the tail, according to Strydom, and there's no bites on her. The door was closed, you said?"

"Completely. I even wondered for a moment if her light was on, and I remember glancing at the edge to see if—"

"Light? Was that on, Marais?"

"Yes, it was on. I noticed because there's no window and—"

"Actually, it was off for a bit," Stevenson confessed. "Every penny counts and—"

"Shut up!"

"You never let me finish a—"

"Take him to his office, for Christ's sake," ordered Kramer.

While Marais was away, Kramer began a careful search of the room. He found two Gunstone butts in a corner, a dress-shirt button with a fancy design under the basin, and nothing to suggest the divan had ever been used for anything except as a place to put the snake basket.

"Who smokes Gunstone filter-tip?" he asked Marais on his return. "You?"

"Ja, sir, but I chucked them both— Where's that button from?"

"That's the first of your problems," Kramer said, handing it to him. "The second is why, with all this bloody mess— powder everywhere, lipsticks without their tops, eyelashes stuck to the mirror, coffee spilled on the hot plate . . . you see what I mean?"

"Sir?"

"I want to know why I've just noticed that she washes a mug and glass nicely and then leaves them on a box that's got jam smeared on it."

"Man, oh, man," Marais murmured. "I didn't think."

"Thirdly, I want Stevenson's alibi for what he did here on the night fully investigated. Get hold of that club member he showed to the door."

Kramer was surprised to find his anger had gone—and

reasoned this was because he had been as much to blame in making these oversights.

"What sort of inquiry is this?" Marais asked. "Has it—er—changed?"

"Not all that much, from what I can see, but if he was in there when it happened, that's a further piece of false information."

"But Stevenson seems—"

"Marais! Just do it, hey? Get Gardiner here, too. I'll take the bugger back on foot and have him locked up for the night. If you want me, use the radio. Okay?"

"Peacevale again, sir?"

"You never know," answered Kramer, and he went down the passage into the office.

Stevenson looked different.

"Been on the phone, have you?" Kramer asked lightly. "Been giving your lawyer a bell? Who is he?"

"Ben Gold—"

"Ben? Hell, it'll be good to hear from an old mate again. But meantime, let's go and see if we have got a nice cell for you."

Stevenson took a little time finding his feet. While this was going on, Kramer noticed a bottle on top of the safe, and that there was only one used tumbler beside it.

Every lie had to start with a truth somewhere, he mused on the way out.

"That's as much as I can ascertain from the outside," said Bose, glancing up from the viper he was painting. "Have you made your mind up yet?"

Strydom dithered, and then closed the door behind him.

"So it wasn't necessarily my boy? She could have done it herself? Are you sure?"

"The possibility must exist. Although it would have had to be coincidental with her own demise."

"Ja, ja—otherwise she could have freed herself."

"May I?" Bose asked deferentially, as one expert does to another before straying into his field.

"Please."

"The reptile could, of course, have been used to cover the—if I may make so bold—the work or rather marks left by another lethal agent. Hmmmm?"

"Manual, you mean? That's where I've just been—to the mortuary to check."

"I see; so that's out of the question. You must pardon my being so fanciful; it's the books my wife reads."

"Agatha Christie?" Strydom asked with interest. "Or Dick Francis?"

"Edward McBain. An American gentleman, I fear. But your decision?"

Strydom dithered again, agonizingly. By rights, he should not be fooling around with an exhibit before the inquest, and it should be safe under lock and key. But then the paper he had planned was a once-in-a-lifetime chance to really impress his colleagues in forensic medicine—colleagues who had, although not perfect themselves, much enjoyed one or two small errors of his in the past. While an actual, life-size model of the python would certainly be the talk of the week.

"So," he said, "it comes down to a coincidence, ja?"

"Nothing more sinister than that," Bose said, with one of his slow smiles.

"But do you—"

"Academic, purely academic interest. The real problem being, if you want it done in a hurry before anyone notices, we'd better make a start. The mold should be allowed to dry for at least a night. I'll pop in a wee bit of salt and speed it up, of course."

"Okay, so we take a chance," Strydom said, getting to the door before adding, "I'm very grateful, hey? If ever you want a special favor done, you know where to come."

The whisper was that Chainpuller Mabatso was running a ruthless protection racket.

But Zondi had tired of whispers. Now he wanted to hear the rest loud and clear from one of the victims. So he pointed his gun, cocked it, and threatened to put a second hole through about two hundred pop songs.

Beebop Williams, sitting around the back of his record bar with his shoelaces tied together, found his voice.

"Must have been two hours after I opened up again," he disclosed earnestly, "when I noticed this cat picking over the latest, but never once did he seek a request. Quite a few folk drove over after the shooting, just to look around—you know, the fat cats from over the top side?"

He meant the black merchants rich enough to have managers run their businesses.

"So I was attending to their needs, and my boy Jerry was helping me out, because when they get excited they don't mind spending money, and so it went for quite a time. Then this guy comes over and says he's got a little deal to discuss, and we come back in here."

"Here?"

"No, man, I can see he's clean—not even a knife," said Williams, at last settling for English, which would be less confusing than a mixture. "But I stand in the doorway, see? Sort of half on. Then he tells me. The butcher wasn't paying up right. He wasn't doing what he should, seeing as he's got this contract."

"Did he say Chainpuller?" Zondi broke in.

Beebop Williams flinched. "That word's on your tongue, brother, and it's ideal—but I didn't put it there. Are we agreed?"

Zondi nodded.

"Then he says his boss is now one short on his contracts and he figures that Beebop is just the man for the job."

"How much?"

"Ten rand a week."

"And did he say anything about Lucky and the others?"

"He kind of waved his hand around. So I got the message."

"The guy that came here—he is coming back for the money?"

Beebop patted to show how flat his pockets were.

"One payment already? How about the rest?"

"Put it like the others in a tin, go up near his—near the hut, and throw."

"When?"

"Sunday night when there's no people around. Now look, man, I don't want no pigs—"

"What did the guy look like? Know his name?"

It nearly came out, then the heat of the moment cooled.

"What guy?" Beebop Williams said, all surprised.

But that was enough. Even the softening effects of sophistication had their limit, and it was time now to contact the lieutenant.

Marais was confident of one thing: the button had not been

80

lost off any of Monty Stevenson's work shirts.

Mrs. Stevenson had emptied the wardrobe shelves for him, and they had ticked off each and every garment against an inventory she kept to inhibit the wash girl's congenital dishonesty. Then there had been tears in the hall—during which Marais learned that whatever happened to Monty didn't matter much, but she'd just realized how she and poor little Jeremy might suffer—and that had been that.

Now he was on his way to interview the last member known to have left the club that night, having decided that the poser of the clean glasses would be best left to a fresh start in the morning. He was light-headed through lack of decent sleep.

It was six o'clock by the time he drove onto the forecourt of the garage. With the law prohibiting the sale of petrol at night and over the weekend, it looked deserted until he noticed a light still burning in the small office to the rear of the showroom.

There Gilbert Littlemore turned out to be one of those ex-Kenya types who kept calling coons "Sambo" and "nig-nog" and other childish names. The sort who made Marais's membership in the Nationalist party seem ridiculous when they twisted apartheid to mean having polite servants and not separate development for all races—which was far more important to anyone who loved the country. Trust throw-out Englishmen to think that politeness was something you needed a policy to control.

"You don't take any of their damn cheek, I suppose?" Littlemore said, pushing aside the hire-purchase forms he had been completing. "I'm sorry to go on like this, but I did expect a bit more discipline down here. Good God, at the rate we're going, I'm likely to find myself working with Jungle Jim alongside of me! As a salesman, I mean!"

"Jungle Jim?" queried Marais, deliberately needling him. That was another thing he couldn't stand—the way they kept trying to be what they thought was South African.

"Oh, my mistake! Jim Fish—that's it, isn't it? Now, you were saying . . .?"

"I'm making certain inquiries concerning the Wigwam, as I told you on the phone, and I would like to have a statement from you."

"Public or private use? Ha-ha!"

81

"Ha, bloody ha," said Marais wearily, getting out his ball-point.

"Well, I was there with a party actually, but they all toddled off before Eve's second performance because one of the ladies said it made her come all over peculiar."

"Or was it you?" Marais said in Afrikaans.

"What? Oh, sorry, can't understand a word of it yet; a jolly bad show, I know."

Just as Marais had supposed. Christ, even Mickey could speak it fluent, and English, too, for that matter, and he was only a wog. But he was on duty and would have to stop playing games and behave himself.

"*Ach,* my mistake, as you say. But can we get to the point, please? When did you see Stevenson?"

"Ah. Seeing I was left alone at the table, the manager came over—Monty, that's right—came across and sat with me. We saw the show, then quietly killed the rest of the wine together. Then he started making noises about licensing hours and, rather unnecessarily, I thought, saw me to the door. After all, we had stopped drinking, and I wasn't going to ruin his carpet for him! Remember saying to him, 'Steady on, old chap, only twenty past—you can't throw a knight out on a dog like this!' Picked that one up in Dar."

Marais, for his part, would have left it there.

"Well, Sergeant, any good to you?"

But Marais was so tired by then that this indication of Stevenson's innocence hardly meant a thing. Except more problems.

Kramer stopped the Chev for only three seconds before roaring off again, saving Zondi any problems in getting the passenger door slammed shut.

Then they laughed together as they often did when first meeting up.

Zondi began by reassuring him that all was well at Blue Haze, and that the children were very pleased with it, and then related his discoveries from the time of seeing Yankee Boy Msomi at the railway station. That gave them a great deal to discuss.

"Okay, so I'm biased," Kramer said eventually, "but all this explains is why they didn't go for big-money places. It wasn't the till they were interested in—that was just a cover-up."

"It also explains why the people say they see nothing. If they hear that Chainpuller is listening, then we stand no chance."

"That's the part that contradicts, Zondi. All these years I've been hearing how Chainpuller can knock the ding-dongs off a bloke at forty yards by just scratching on the wall—and now suddenly he needs gangsters, guns, cars. Why?"

"I have another thought: maybe this gang is *using* Chainpuller, boss."

"Hey, just wait. Another part that contradicts is that at Lucky's place you told me the minister was a good bugger. Would he believe all this crap about wizards, too?"

Zondi shrugged as if religion and superstition had never been separate in his view.

"But you were saying . . . ?"

"Yes, boss, it is the way the money's paid. One of these *skabengas* could hide there in the grass and catch the tins that are thrown. That's how I mean by using Chainpuller."

Kramer smiled and said, "I take my hat off to them, then—at least *they* can't be so poop-scared of him!"

Which was another point that Zondi had evidently not considered, and so they went back to the first theory again.

Until Kramer brought the Chev to a halt, made a U-turn on the Kwela Village road, and started back the other way.

"So we go to find the guy who came in the shop," Zondi said with satisfaction. "Beebop will talk to you, boss—you know his type."

"I'm not sodding round when I can go to the top," Kramer replied. "That bastard Chainpuller has had things his way for too bloody long."

And not without reason, suggested the silence at his side.

The rain began again, softly. Freckling over the windshield and then making Marais switch on the wipers.

He leaned forward to see better, cursing the sting of his eyes, and regretting having accepted that drink from Little-more. Scotch gave him heartburn.

The street was oily with colors from the shopwindows and illuminated signs on either side of it. Cars cruised slowly, looking for parking places, and sodding well getting in his way. The route he had chosen was the shortest between the garage and the CID building, but perhaps it might have been quicker to go a longer way round.

One sign, he noted, was out. Nobody was being enticed up the alley to Wiggle at the Wigwam Tonite.

"*Ach,* ja," Marais said to himself. He had known there was method in his madness: he'd promised Gardiner to check by on the way back, mainly so they could have a drink together.

Driving much more slowly, he passed the entrance to the alley and saw a group of people standing there. That was odd. Mrs. Stevenson had surely thought to cancel any reservations, and he himself had pinned up a CLOSED sign on the door.

Ghouls! The boss had left strict instructions about how they were to be treated.

Marais left his car double-parked with the flasher going, and sprinted across.

"Okay, what's going on here?" he demanded.

Indians all dressed up in bow ties and mackintoshes turned in alarm at the sound of the familiar phrase, making him blink disbelief until he identified them as waiters. Then a short white man in a ginger beard and wearing a sheepskin jacket came from the back of them.

"That's what we want to know!"

"Who are you?"

"Could ask the same!"

"Police, so watch it. What's the problem?"

"We turn up for work and sign says the joint's closed. Nobody told us. Why and for how long? We've—"

"Owner's under arrest," said Marais.

The man grinned and said, "Hear that, boys? What did I tell you?"

The Indians smiled.

"You told them what?"

"Monty definitely had a finger in that pie," the man replied, smirking at his witticism.

"You'd say—"

"Man, what are you? Security Branch? I'm not giving away secrets—everyone knows what a two-faced bastard he is!"

Everybody then decided to leave the pair of them alone.

"Give my love to Minnehaha!" the man called after them, and this time got his laugh. From a safe distance.

"Monty's squaw," the man explained. "Him we call Big Chief Running Guts—or Hiya Sexy! Depends."

"You're the funny man in the show?"

"Me? I'm the tickler. Pianist. Y'know. Drums and sax were here, but they've gone over the road to get pissed."

"Name?"

"Bix Johnson. And you?"

"Marais, CID."

"I'm BA."

"Hey?"

The street, it seemed, was no place to hold an intelligent conversation.

"Are you prepared to assist in some inquiries? If you're not, then I'll want to know why and I'll—"

"How much do you pay?"

"Who?"

"You know something? You're terrific! Unreal! Oi, oi, oi. For you, I do dis for nuttin."

"What?"

"You ask, I'll tell. Easy as that. Where's your motor? What do you say—can we make a move, Captain?"

They made a move. And then they made surprisingly good friends. Bix Johnson had a way with him that gave Marais an entirely new lease of energy.

He also gave him some information that had Marais on the radio, calling urgently for Lieutenant Kramer.

But answer came there none.

7

They made a startling sound in the dead of night. Within seconds the caretaker was out in the hall with a gun shaking in his hand.

Then, when he saw the empty milk bottles rolling about, and who had knocked them over, he quickly lowered the revolver before there could be an accident.

"Heaven's sakes, laddie, but you gave me a terrible turn!" he said.

Kramer admired the old bugger's courage and alertness, but wondered if he hadn't been drinking—then saw his teeth were missing.

"*Ach,* sorry, Mr. McKay. I was backing up and I didn't notice them by the door."

"Your boy should have warned you," McKay said, just to show there were no hard feelings. "Still at it, then? Thought you'd finished before lunch."

And he nodded at the burden Kramer and Zondi were carrying between them, peering short-sightedly in an effort to make out what was wrapped inside the car tarpaulin.

"Some bits of carpet from upstairs that didn't suit the new place, so she thought the new tenants might like to at least see if they wanted them. They can always chuck them out."

"But they're not moving in until the day after—"

"I realize," said Kramer, "but you know what womenfolk are like in this mood—they can't stop till it's all done."

McKay showed gum and sympathized. "I ken fine! I ruddy dread new arrivals—Mr. McKay this, Mr. McKay that. The worst are the ones who think your name's Jock and that you're responsible for the dirty books their bairns find left under the bath."

Zondi gave Kramer a pleading look.

"We better be going, Mr. McKay. Mustn't hold you up."

"A wee moment—the keys?"

"Tomorrow?"

"Aye, fine; no hurry, no hurry. Then I'll be wishing you a good night."

He hobbled back into his flat and Zondi immediately pushed toward the lift, making Kramer nearly start the whole thing up again outside the door to number 1B.

That had been their worst moment. The actual abduction of Chainpuller Mabatso had run like clockwork, while observing to the letter a strict condition Zondi had placed upon it. All they had done was to sneak down the ridge behind the hut, arrange themselves with the tarpaulin on one side of the door, toss up a cocoa tin with some change in it, and wait. Chainpuller had meandered out, buttoning up his fly, and had been engulfed as he stooped to recover his dues.

And the best moment had been when Chainpuller's current rental, all straight-haired wig and white lipstick, had poked her head out to see the wizard of Peacevale being carried off by two demons without faces—a sleeve of cheesecloth, thoughtfully provided by Bokkie Howells for cleaning the car's windows, had been easily divided into two masks that didn't even need eyeholes. While the story she'd tell would be half the battle won already.

Kramer groaned and took a grip on the heavy end again as the lift opened at the fifth floor. As lightweight as Chainpuller might prove on a set of scales, having to lug him all the way up the ridge and then down the other side, to where their car was hidden, had been enervating as well as time-consuming.

"Last lap," he said to Zondi, "and for Christ's sake don't step on that cat."

Strydom sat up in bed panting. His wife's plump arm encircled his waist and tried to pull him down again as she muttered endearments. But he stayed where he was, tense and in a muck sweat.

"What is it, Chris?" she finally asked, rousing herself to lie propped on one elbow.

"I don't know."

"You haven't had a dream, hey? You never have dreams—since when did you have a dream? I've never known you to have dreams. Never."

87

"Hmmm?"

"I mean, with your work you can't afford to—at least, that's what you've always said. Remember? That time on our honeymoon when I thought you were dreaming? Only it was me dreaming that you were dreaming and all the time you—"

"It was terrible!"

"Hey?"

"No, I meant . . . it must have been a dream. So lifelike and real, though. Right in front of me. With smells, too."

"You get smells in dreams sometimes," she replied reassuringly, taking his clenched hand and patting it. "And colors? Did you see colors as well?"

"Ja, I did. Isn't it supposed to be black and white, like the newsreels?"

"Not always. Although last time mine was black and white and I was trying on new dresses and it nearly drove me mad. Maybe it was that book you were reading."

"No."

"*Ach,* tell your little Anneline all about it, and then it'll go away. Come on, Chrissy, lie down again beside me."

He lay back, hearing the mattress sigh with him, and moved his head over until he could feel her white curls against his cheek.

"Man, it was terrible," he said in a low whisper. "I was back in Pretoria Central on a morning of some hangings. Father William was there, and Koos and the commandant—all the usual crowd."

"Go on, my pet."

"Things were going just as normal, and I had this feeling I had been away but was pleased to see everyone again. Only I couldn't see the hangman and I wanted to ask him how his racing pigeons were coming on. I kept looking for him although work had already piled up for me downstairs—"

"They'd started with the Bantu?"

"Ja, although that didn't seem funny at the time. Six Bantu and a colored, two rapes and the rest murder—no, one housebreaking with aggravated circumstances. Anyway, I knew there were all those certificates to sign. So I thought maybe he is in the condemned cell in B2, the small one for Europeans. I went there and I could tell which one from the aromas of the steak and eggs the bloke had ordered. You remember? Nearly always steak and eggs and peaches for pudding—hell, I was the one who actually saw all that food go to waste. But here am I outside the cell, and I push the thing back and look in. You know what I see there? A big mirror on the wall and my eye looking back at me. That's the first thing I see."

"And that's what gave you such a big fright?"

"*Ach*, no—wait. When I take my head away, I'm not by the cell anymore, I'm back in the shed. Of course, I think, this is where he'll be. But I'm just there by myself. Then they bring in the white prisoner and I see that it's Tromp!"

"Who?"

"Tromp Kramer—and I know this even though he's already got the black hood on. Everything's quick so I can't ask about the pigeons and they put him on the trap and Father William says the Amen and he's hanging—hell, but the bugger kicked hard! And I see . . . you know how the chain comes over the beam to make different lengths for the rope? You know that chart I showed you, heights and weights and the slack in between? I look up to see if it's holding because I don't want him to suffer—that's rubbish for you, the chain coming loose."

"Ja—"

"And all of a sudden I see it's a mamba, not a rope, and that it's—"

Anneline Strydom laughed fondly, replacing her arm and hugging her husband to her.

"You're so silly," she said. "Anyone can see where this dream came from. You don't need Joseph to tell you it would just break, do you? Trompie jumped, he was all right—and you know how that boy likes his big plates of steak and eggs. Remember that time? I'd made for four?"

He laughed and snuggled up.

Gardiner was doodling. Drawing cartoon faces on thumbprints he had himself made on the back of an old calendar, and giving them legs. Then he gave them arms and different things to hold, and wrote funny captions beneath each one, like "I never laid a finger on her" and "My alibi is I was out hitchhiking." He had always liked art, even the watercolors at junior school, which always ran into each other, and his considerable graphic skill had made his specialized branch of police work a wise and rewarding choice.

Gardiner was also waiting. Marais had rung him in high excitement to ask if anything dramatic had been found in the dressing room, and when told it hadn't, the clown promised to be over in a tick. He apparently had something momentous to impart, once he'd finished writing it out neatly for the lieutenant.

But the wait was getting beyond a joke. Both Gardiner's dinner and his pretty wife would be stone cold by the time he got home, and he'd been hoping to broach the matter of a fishing trip up the North Coast instead of the visit to the game reserve.

So he finally just locked up and went over to the CID building, noticing the time on the city hall clock and discovering that his watch had lost an hour. This very nearly made him pick up the car and go, but his curiosity, as always, got the better of him. His rank had been well earned.

Marais was asleep, his head resting on folded arms on top of his typewriter. The snoring would have done justice to a bullfrog.

Gardiner saw the sheet of paper in the machine had just been begun, so he picked up what looked like a first draft and found it was, in fact, a formal statement written in an almost illegible hand by one Benjamin "Bix" Harold Johnson. Marais would never learn.

Yet once it was understood that the *r*'s were really *m*'s and that a dot served for a *the,* the thing flowed quite reasonably. Skipping the address, race, and age bit, Gardiner hooked a leg over the desk corner to read the rest.

The gig ended at 12 A.M. sharp and the Club Manager, MONTY STEVENSON, was there to see the Customers didn't dilly-dally. I observed Stevenson at a table with a person known to me as GILBERT, a Car Salesman. Us boys in the band had been bought drinks by one of the grateful, and so we were entitled to drink them as we had not had time before. THEO HILL, who plays the tenor saxophone, and MAC TAYLOR, drums, share a pad and a Volksy.

These two colleagues said good night to me at 12:10 or thereabouts, and went straight out through the front because of some nurses on nights having supper at one. I had promised some of the Staff a lift to the bottom end of town and was waiting for them to finish in the Kitchen. One of them approached me and asked if he could see the cassette Player he heard I had for sale. This Person was an Indian Male by the name of RAMCHUNDER who I call RAM because his first name is too hard to pronounce. The Boss was busy so he did not notice Ramchunder and me sneak into the passage to the dressing rooms. As a nonwhite, Ramchunder was out of bounds in this area, but I wanted to save myself the bother of going back and forward and the others thinking I had gone.

We therefore proceeded quietly to the Second Dressing Room where the Trio keeps its gear like scores and novelty instruments. I observed the Door to the First Dressing Room, in use at the time by the Deceased, SONJA BERGSTROOM, was closed and bolted. It had to be, because it was our old dressing room and if it wasn't bolted the Door hung open slightly even after you had pushed it hard. This did not strike me in any way as strange as I knew the Deceased must be changing and packing. She was not a friendly type so I didn't greet her as we passed. In fact, because RAMCHUNDER was with me, we went by almost on tiptoe so there would be no fuss.

There was no light in the Second Dressing Room as the switch had been broken for weeks, so Ramchunder inspected the Player by the light from the Passage. As it still had its "silica gel" packet, he said he would take it straight away if he could have it on installments. At this stage we heard Raised Voices in the Dressing Room next door, one of which I recognized as being that of the Deceased. The other was a Male Voice I did not recognize although I was interested and tried to. RAMCHUNDER then pointed out it would be best if we struck a bargain in the Car because there was a danger of him being seen Out of Bounds by whoever this was.

We then left, taking the Player with us, and as we passed the Door to the First Dressing Room we head a Laugh that seemed too Hoarse to have been made by the Deceased and she always pretended what a lady she was and prim. Upon reentering the dance and cabaret area, I observed that STEVENSON had still not got rid of GILBERT. The Others were waiting by this time and we all went out the Front Way. The back way is never used because it is blocked by a Freezer in Contravention of Fire Regulations as I have Informed the Manager. As we got to the street, I again heard a Laugh. I turned to see who was laughing and saw STEVENSON in the distance at the entrance to the Club with a Male Figure I did not recognize in a Coat. I cannot be certain the laugh was the same one as had been made in the Dressing Room (First) but I thought the Male Figure could be the same one. I think it was 12:20 or thereabouts because the persons with me wanted to reach their Destination at 12:30 and we made it easily on time. It does usually take Ten Minutes to get the car and go there. That is all I can think of.

Gardiner dropped the statement and picked up another signed by Gilbert Edward Littlemore. One by one the pennies began to drop, making an interesting sound.

The silence was almost more stifling than the foul air he breathed.

Chainpuller Mabatso had listened to it for more than half the night, by his reckoning. Once or twice he had thought he heard a baby bawling, and there had been strange sounds like a club hitting a metal pipe. That he could not understand.

Nor could he understand the flatness of the surface upon which he was lying. He had not been on anything so hard and smooth since the concrete bunk he had slept in at the penal colony. It was this sensation, above all, that had kept him motionless so long. Ever since he had awakened from a sleep with a headache and a pain in his stomach. He felt as though he had kneed himself because his knee hurt also.

He thought back. He had been in his hut with the new woman. The one who wanted to put her mouth on his mouth like a European. Then, while he was telling her of his disgust, there had been the clunk of one of his tins arriving. He had gone out and bent down and . . .

Surely he was not dead.

Mabatso tried to move and found the cord that bound him had been loosely tied. He worked his hands free and tried to get them to his mouth to take out a piece of rag he had first imagined the laying-out woman had put there. But the shroudlike wrapping was on too tight. He tried rolling on his side, and then the other way, and this worked. He sat up and looked around him.

The hut had flat, flat walls, narrow planks of wood nailed along near the top where the roof was even flat, and a window made of one big piece of glass. And a door.

He had never seen anything like it.

Yes, he had: the police station where he had been taken as a youth. Only that had been full of tables and chairs and other things that showed its purpose. This place had none.

A giddiness made him rock for a moment, then it passed.

Mabatso undid the bow tied in the cord around his ankles and then, stiffly and cautiously, moved onto his feet. He wobbled, holding his arms out at his sides, and then shuffled forward in a crouch.

He heard a car in the distance. And saw moonlight.

Moving like a river crab, he made his way toward the window, careful not to make a sound, and slid his fingertips up the wall to the window ledge. He had to know what kind of place lay outside.

Very, very warily, he moved his whole body up from the floor until his eyes cleared the sill tiles.

Then Chainpuller Mabatso sobbed and drew himself into a tight ball, rolling over and hiding his face in his hands, keeping his sobs silent.

There was nothing outside. The hut hung in the sky.

Kramer would not have continued up the drive if a light hadn't come on in the living room. The curtains were wrong, so he saw quite clearly that the Widow Fourie had gone to read a book in the corner.

He deliberately made a slightly noisy arrival, and waved to her when she hurried to the window.

"Oh, Trompie, Trompie," she said, embracing him as he stepped onto the veranda—which was not like her.

"What's the matter, hey? Is it Piet?"

"Man, I've been so worried. He was so happy today, you should have seen him, exploring and making the others play his games, and then just now he starts . . ."

Kramer led her back into the living room and made her

93

settle back in her chair. Then he poured two brandies from the bottle she had waiting for him and clinked his glass against hers.

"Blue Haze," he said.

"Trompie . . ."

"Piet's not good tonight?"

"I thought at first it was having a room all to himself. And the move—that always upsets some kids, doesn't it? Of course, the others settled down like lambs, except I had to go in and kiss them about four hundred times. And oh, the two smallest have stayed together. But Piet! He suddenly woke up and started screaming and he won't tell me why. I've been trying to look it up."

Kramer took the book from her and saw it was *The Rib Cage: A Study in Child Development and Certain Problems*. It was the same one he had quoted from most extensively, and yet she had been foolish enough to go out and buy her own copy.

"*Ach*, but this is bullsugar!" he said, hoping for an easy laugh.

"What's so wrong with it?"

"I can't even understand the bloody title for a bloody start, so what chances do I stand with the rest of it?"

"You know—Adam's rib, women, the cages that mothers make for their children, imprisoning them in their own whatsits."

"Ja, exactly!" Kramer retored. "Whatsits. Thingummies. All these big new words. And how's old He's-a-poof?"

"There's nothing the matter with the Oedipus complex," the Widow Fourie said crossly. "All it means is a boy gets jealous of his dad and this makes him feel afraid he's having such thoughts. Piet isn't the only kid who's ever said to his mum that she's the one girl he likes. And when he says that, he doesn't say it the way you might do."

"Have I ever?" he asked.

"True enough!" she replied, and could not help a twinkle. "But the doctors didn't say Piet had that anyway."

"I should bloody hope not! You know what this book alleges? It alleges that is how psychopaths are made."

The Widow Fourie set down her brandy. Her day had been a long one, too.

"Listen, before you start telling me everything, why don't

94

you take the trouble to read it up properly? Oedipus is only part of psychopathetics, and it's to do with their consciences. They don't feel guilty and they don't feel sorry for others—why? Because they don't have a mum's care and attention when they are small—say, until so high. I've got the place right here—it's in the beginning. Now listen: 'If early rearing is unstable and transi—transient, then empathy fails to'—*hey!*"

Kramer, who already had one leg in the corridor, and a lot else still to do that night, said, "Just hang on a sec while I go and chuck him some bananas."

The book just missed.

Mabatso had drunk very nearly a gallon of maize beer before being spirited away. He was now acutely uncomfortable and knew something would have to be done about it.

So he made his second move, less afraid now because of various ideas he had slowly assembled. But he crawled all the way to the window, and didn't open his eyes until he was standing before it.

Then he saw the houses down below and the streetlights and the milk trolley's lantern, and swayed. It was the first time he had ever been higher off the ground than the roof of his hut when it needed mending, and this took some adjustment. After a time, he stopped swaying.

And turned to explore the room with the hope of finding somewhere he could do it. He had learned in the colony what happened to men who relieved themselves on a white man's floor.

But the only thing in the room which resembled an outlet was a flat plate, with three small holes in it, screwed so low on the wall he could not get near it.

So finally he was forced to take hold of the door handle and, with a shuddering breath, turn it. Nothing happened as he opened the door a little way. . . . He opened his eyes again and breathed out. It was another empty room, only there were four doors opening off it, two of which stood ajar.

Mabatso scurried across into the nearest of these, saw it was for cooking and that there were taps. The sink was reached just in time.

Now he felt able to think properly.

He looked in through the other open doorway, recognized

95

the shower—the colony had had several—and felt confident enough to try the other doors. One wouldn't open, and one led into a third room, as large as the first, with glass right down to the floor on the far side.

"Ee-flat," he said to himself, remembering the word used by a fellow convict who had worked in one. It was all making sense now. What a fool he had been. Excellent sense.

Up to a point.

And when Mabatso's thoughts reached that point, the giddiness returned twice as violently as before, dropping him to his knees with a jolt. To crumple once again and lie there, curled up like a wood louse, smelling his own smells among so many sharp alien smells, and feeling more afraid than he had ever done.

Because when those colony gates had swung open, he'd not only known what sort of place it was, but also how he had reached it, why he was there, and what to expect while he remained behind its walls.

Whereas now he knew the answer to only the first of those questions, and the rest of them had begun to tease his mind apart.

Chainpuller Mabatso could not even cry out. As isolated as his life had been on that hillside, he fully realized that a black man always had to have a very good reason for being in a white people's dwelling at night.

Which came to the same terrifying thing.

Ramchunder had a rude awakening. His bedding was stripped off him and a flashlight shone in his eyes.

"CID. On your feet," said Marais.

The waiter staggered up.

"Are you awake, man?"

"I—yes, I am, sir."

"Have you in your possession a cassette player recently bought?"

"Have merciful pity, sir! The gent I bought it from said he had come by it quite aboveboard."

"You're making allegations?"

"Sir, you misinterpret!"

"*Ach*, all right, Sammy—just as long as you're the right Ramchunder," said Marais, who had unearthed a good dozen of the buggers, all of them waiters.

96

Then he took a short statement which tallied in every particular with the one given to him by Bix Johnson, the crazy piano player. And had problems only when it came to Ramchunder's reluctance to admit having been through the curtain.

"Do I go up for trespass?" Ramchunder asked gloomily as the ballpoint was put away.

"Not this time," said Marais, and his good humor made him add, "That's one of your boss's laws, not mine!"

Kramer talked man-to-man with Piet until the little sod toppled sideways and fell fast asleep. Then he tucked a rug over the Widow Fourie, closed the padlock on the burglar guard at the front door, and drove back into Trekkersburg.

Dawn had just begun to snuffle its pink snout along the escarpment when he slipped past Mr. McKay's flat and took the stairs. The lift at that hour sounded like Saturn 5.

By the fifth-floor landing, Kramer had decided there must be easier ways of making a wizard talk. But when he heard the rapid exchange in Zulu coming from behind the living room door of number 5C, he felt it may well have been worth all the extra trouble. And sat down where the coat stand had once been.

He tried to sleep a little. But there was something odd about Zondi's tone that kept snagging on his veil of oblivion —something that made him sit upright and try to distinguish words.

Not long after that, the inner door opened and Kramer saw Zondi standing over him in shirtsleeves.

"Hope you slept well, you bugger," Kramer said, getting up with a spring that sagged in the middle.

"Three, four hours, then this one started to knock for me."

"Oh, ja? And?"

"The truth, I think."

Kramer looked over Zondi's shoulder. What he saw made him realize there was no need to dispute that—although he could also see Mabatso had not a mark on him, nor any reason to have one either.

"All right, but what did he say?"

"The man who asked Beebop for the ten rand was one Robert Zulu, who this prisoner knew in prison, and who work like an errand boy for him, buying him beer and all that. Finish of story."

"Hey? Come on now!"

Zondi smiled in an ugly way and said, "Chainpuller doesn't know any more about the robberies than we. He just got the idea of pretending he was behind them—he was riding the gangsters like a tick."

"Him? This thing? Where did he get ideas like that from? And so quick?"

"Chainpuller does this all the time—for years, boss. You know that brother? He is an important man now, down in the Transkei, so he cuts himself free from this rubbish. But you know how it is when people think you have done a wrong, how they make sure this comes to your ears? Mabatso here was told many things about himself after the brother had gone, and so he—"

"You mean he never did anything to anyone? Just sat on his arse and let people throw their money at him?"

"That is the truth. It was the people's own fears of darkness that made him so great—darkness only in their own minds."

"What are you, Mickey Zondi?"

"I'm a superstitious kaffir," said Zondi, breaking into a wide grin. "And you, boss, are wiser than the elephant.'

"*Ach*, I wouldn't go so far as to say that, hey? But I can tell you one thing: I don't suffer the same way from the blind spots of my people. Not in my work anyway."

That, too, was meant as a joke, something flippant to lighten the disappointment now weighing down hard on both of them. But somehow it seemed to misfire.

Zondi said, "The charge against this prisoner, Lieutenant? Demanding with menaces?"

"Ja, what you like."

It was a great pity the new day had to begin like that, almost as an omen.

8

The museum opened to the public at ten. Strydom arrived at nine and went in through the side entrance. He had not only the overnights to see to at the mortuary, but also both police patients and corporal punishments to attend. In other words, this was his only hour free until evening.

"Oh, there you are," said Bose. "Had the idea of getting everything ready for you before your arrival."

"Sorry, man, but I checked with the magistrate and that didn't take as long as I thought. He says we can go ahead and do what we like. How is he?"

"It's a beauty," Bose declared without pride, as he continued to remove sections of the mold.

The plaster had taken every detail of the scales and Strydom clasped his hands in delight. Bose had coiled the creature in a most realistic manner, and even a layman could see how well this was going to reproduce.

"Might manage a lick of paint," Bose murmured. "We haven't a new case going in for some months yet."

Strydom had already been captivated by the clockless back rooms of the museum, and very nearly asked if they ever employed skilled pensioners on bird stuffing or the like. Then wonder returned his thoughts to the immediate.

"Lovely and shiny," he said.

"Vaseline; prevents it sticking to the p.o.p. The fact the colors fade so rapidly is one of the main reasons we've gone over onto casts. Now, *Python regius,* consent has been given, so it's time for your little operation."

Strydom, who could have kicked himself for not going through the proper channels in the first place, and so saving himself much anxiety, said idly, "King python, is it?"

"Royal. Must have been imported from up north and have cost a pretty penny, too. Although, with proper care, their life span makes it a goodish investment. Very gentle nature; an excellent pet."

"No, thanks!"

"Any animal," Bose reminded him pointedly, with a mischievous smile, "is apt to behave in a strongly defensive manner if it believes itself to be threatened. Usually, our friend the royal makes himself into an almost perfect ball, with his head tucked away on the inside—you can literally roll him about with your foot. Quite a trick."

"Wonder if it was in her act."

"Shouldn't think so; once they're tame, they stop doing it. Excuse me a moment."

The dead reptile was now lying stretched out on its back along the zinc-topped table. Strydom put down his bag and went over to examine the two horny claws just in front of its vent.

"Vestigial hind limbs," Bose explained, unrolling a canvas holder lined with dissecting instruments. "The family *Boidae* have a quite recognizable pelvic girdle, which I'll show you. Males use the claws to stroke the female during courtship—while *they* seem to have no use for them at all."

"Hell, I never thought of them as lovers." Strydom chuckled. In fact, as he realized then, he had lived all his life surrounded by snakes without giving them any thought at all—except, momentarily, while dispatching them with his golf club.

"Nor had I," said Bose, selecting a large scalpel.

But Strydom's curiosity had been aroused. "So how come they lost them? I thought legs were a step up the scale, if you get my meaning!"

"Ah, not much good for burrowing. It's believed that snakes evolved about one and a quarter million years ago from some lizards that took to burrowing, lost the use of their legs, and returned limbless to the surface. There are several other indications of this as well."

Bose was plainly flattered by an attentive pupil, so Strydom decided this would be a good moment to put a question that might have seemed impertinent before.

"I've been wondering, man, why you keep shoving the blame on the girl when how can we be sure that the python didn't attack her in the first place?"

"Aha, the Tarzan fallacy! Come up this end and take a

100

look at the teeth. Notice how big they are and how they point backward—and now contrast them with the two fangs of this viper here."

Strydom did that.

"Neither, you have noted, are designed for chewing. Snakes do not chew their food, but swallow it whole. The nearest thing to mastication is found in the eggeater, known hereabouts as *Dasypeltis scaber*, which has a special downward-pointing projection from its spine that breaks the shell of an engorged meal, allowing it to spit out the bits. But come now—why does the royal have them, do you think?"

There was obviously a catch to this, so Strydom's reply was grudgingly given. "To bite with?"

"Good."

"But I'd already thought of that. She must have just been quicker."

"Quicker than this chap? Contrary to Lord Greystoke's simian beliefs, constrictors begin like any other snake by striking, not by wrapping themselves around you. The teeth are for holding on, for *getting to grips* with their prey. Having secured a hold, then they coil themselves around and try, if they can, to keep their tails anchored to a fixed object in order—"

"I know," said Strydom, "but how hard exactly is the squeeze?"

"Sufficient to cause suffocation by immobilizing the respiratory apparatus. Strangulation may, or may not, come into it, too, but they are certainly not given to crushing anything to a bloody pulp. As pulp fiction would have it!"

Strydom only half heard this afterthought and neglected to smile; he was already anticipating questions from the floor of the conference hall.

"The degree of pressure always interests us," he said. "There have been cases when in orgasm the human male has inadvertently caused the death of the female with his hands. Can you be more specific?"

"Certainly. If you had a small boa in a figure eight around your wrists, it would seem virtually impossible to disengage yourself and your hands would rapidly swell. And I'm speaking in terms of an averagely powerful man. Living handcuffs."

"Or a living ligature," remarked Strydom solemnly, as

Bose slit open the python from chin to tail and peeled back the outer layers of muscle.

"Not as putrid as we thought," the scientist said.

Strydom looked again. Conditioned by years of doing much the same thing to *Homo sapiens*, he had expected to see the same glossy array of paired organs exposed before him in their God-ordained order.

"You've only dealt with frogs, I take it," Bose said, noticing the lift of the thick bushy eyebrows. "This shape is ideal for digestive purposes, being, to all intents, one length of gut, but it does make a rather tight fit otherwise."

"Only one of each?"

"As you say, sometimes only the one. Sometimes they are arranged one behind the other, sometimes the right is much larger and better developed than the left, and, of course, gross elongation comes into it as well. Observe how this lung extends for more than half the length of the body But let me poke about a bit and see if it was your boy or the young lady in her extremis who did the damage."

"Most grateful," said Strydom, now not giving a fig for the time either.

Pedro, the giant tortoise at the Trekkersburg Bird Sanctuary, was said to have shared Napoleon's exile on the island of St. Helena. He looked as if he'd had a hell of a life. There were splashes of egret dropping almost half an inch thick on his black shell, and his mouth had a permanent downward twist to it.

Kramer knew how he felt. He *empathized*.

But decided to wake Zondi all the same. So he got out of the Chev, where he had been dozing uneasily, shook down his trousers to ankle length again, and went across to the bench. It was amazing how the little bugger did it—slept like that, out cold, at the drop of his cocky straw hat, even though the new road system had destroyed the value of the place as a quiet retreat during daylight hours.

Kramer picked up the hat and let the sudden blaze of direct sun burn into the eyelids.

"The bench was comfy, boss," Zondi said, his old self again.

"Uh-huh. And the new car smelled like you said it did."

"You're not so good, then?"

"Worse than you think."

Zondi opened his eyes and sat up. "In what way?" he asked.

"I switched on the radio just now to see if there was anything on the go in Peacevale."

"*Aikona*, no!"

"Relax, all's quiet. But you know that case Sergeant Marais was handling? With the snake? Prisoner's gone and killed himself."

The vertrebrae were exposed.

"Neat, hey?" enthused Strydom.

"Complex ball-and-socket joints, articulation at no fewer than five points."

"No wonder they can twist about."

"Ah, but within limits," said Bose, dissecting cautiously. "Each joint can bend through roughly twenty-five degrees from side to side, but only a few degrees vertically. That's why there are so many of them, like drawing a circle using lots of tiny straight lines. On the vertical axis, it can take only so much of a curve before snapping. Spinal cord gets pinched, spasm follows. . . . Hmmm."

Strydom craned forward to see better.

"Just a moment, Doctor. We mustn't nick ourselves."

Bose excised a section of the spine and placed it under the special light he used for painting—which had the same color temperature, whatever that meant, as the neon strips in the cases.

"Now use the glass yourself," he said to Strydom, handing it over. "You'll see the cord has actually been torn apart; not pinched but—"

"Ja, I see—the same as a banger in a Christmas cracker."

"So that's your boy exonerated. I had thought, when you said you were hard pushed for space, that he might have overdone things and effected a fracture in that way. But I doubt very much he would have played tug o' war with it."

"Oh, no. Not him. He's a good worker, never fools around."

"Then we're back to the unfortunate young woman. She must have had an exceptional pair on her."

"Hey?"

"To pull—or counterpull—like that. Quite a lengthy battle

it must have been, but I think I can provide you with a respectable explanation for your forensic colleagues."

"Oh, ja?"

"Do point out to them that snakes are incapable of their legendary capacity for swift cross-country sorties in pursuit of game rangers," Bose said. "The truth is they easily tire, due to their blood's slow rate of oxygenation. Terribly sluggish, if I may use the term. As to top speeds, I would put a mamba's best sprint at somewhere around the four-miles-an-hour mark, but that's rather a tangent."

"I get you! Bergstroom's pulling one way, to bring it round and get it off, but it's pulling the other way in panic and just for one second it starts to go flop and boomph!"

Bose nodded slowly after due consideration, and then replied, "Would you like me to draft out a more detailed exposition, for inclusion, say, as a footnote?"

"Man, would I appreciate that? Please. But for how long would this have gone on? A minute?"

His mentor politely hid a smile but the big gray eyes leaked it.

"The metabolism of *Python regius* is not altogether quite as . . ." Bose paused and rephrased: "The process of suffocation by constriction is always fairly prompt, and yes, as you say, three or four minutes would or could be sufficient. But I'd imagine, with regard to a struggle, it would take at least five times as long to exhaust him."

Strydom did the sum, then saw the dressing room quite vividly in his mind's eye: while it was messy and untidy and nothing was in its proper place, it certanly showed no sign of a prolonged struggle. Why, there was the stool, right beside the body, and still upright. The mirror wasn't straight, but seemed to have been put up that way.

Then somehow he was led on to think the unthinkable.

The colonel had broken his plastic ruler. He placed the halves of it on either side of his blotter and took up the note.

"Where did he get pencil and paper?" he asked Kramer.

"Off Ben, who was acting for him."

"This was last night? Late?"

"Uh-huh, in the cell."

"What was the nature of their conversation?"

"Stevenson hoped Ben could get him off the charges. Says

he kept asking for it to be settled out of court, like a civil case or something. Ben explained the difference, said he'd have to appear in court today to be remanded, but it wouldn't take long and he'd get bail. Asked Ben if the press boys would be there, and Ben told him you could never tell—and it wasn't any good trying to bribe them."

"You would not have opposed bail?"

"By this time, Marais was in possession of fresh information. Did you know—"

"Later, Tromp; this first. I've got to ring Ben Goldstein myself. Already the widow is onto us for 'unlawful harassment' of her husband. What the hell did you do at his place yesterday? Now the maid there says she overheard you threatening him with a broomstick!"

"Fairy stories. And as for his wife, she despises his guts."

"She doesn't have to anymore, Kramer. She can just cherish a dear, sweet memory of him. That's trouble you've been in before."

Uh-huh."

"Pleased with yourself, hey? Then you take another look—here!"

Colonel Muller dropped the note into Kramer's lap as he stalked across to the window.

On one side the thing read in neat, but progressively heavier writing:

I am sick of who you think you are. I will *NOT* take orders to stand up in court and face that kind of publicity. Why should I? I'll show you I can still be a free man. I'm only sorry for Jeremy.

And, on the reverse side, in thin, hasty loops:

Why not ask Shirley, Lt. Kramer? Maybe it's too late for me to remember that now though!!! M.S.

So Stevenson had seen that the pen was a sword that cuts both ways, Kramer noted with a smile.

"Now it's a laughing matter!" the colonel exploded. "You've got him crapping himself so hard that the last thing he does is try and bloody cooperate! He scribbles that on the back and then what? He takes his stinking socks and ties

105

knots in them and stuffs them down his throat! They tell me he must have pushed them as far as his finger could reach. God in heaven!"

"Ja, but I think it was him puking up behind them that made the wool seal off tight," Kramer muttered, staring at the last line again.

"Where's the district surgeon? That's his job!"

"Nobody knows, sir. Wife says he had a bad night."

"Huh! My heart bleeds. Whatever happens, see he knows about the conference at eleven. I want you, the DS, and Marais all here on the dot!"

"Look, meantime I'll give Sam a bell for you," Kramer said, rather than offered. "This is my doing, so there's no need for you to worry."

And he left the room, with the colonel staring suspiciously after him, saying for the umpteenth time, "God in heaven." As first guesses go, it went. Shirley was not Mrs. Stevenson's first name; hers was Trudy. Then Winifred Amelia.

"Fly me to Miami," said Bix Johnson, mystifying Marais. Who had asked him to show him where things were kept at the Wigwam.

"Then we'll just have to go through the whole list of members," Marais said, still showing imagination. "He's the sort of bloke who uses first names in preference, am I right?"

"He does, he does."

Marais was pleased with his clever use of the present tense; he needed the piano player's spite kept alive for a while yet.

"And yet you are sure he didn't have any women friends or acquaintances by that name?"

"You must be joking, Sarge. Only got Eve to sit with him because he was the boss."

"*Ach,* look—it's only initials," Marais complained, flipping over the pages of the membership roll.

"Upsy—a page back. There you are: Shirley."

"And it's *Mr.,* so it must be a bloke.'

"Quick!" said the enigmatic Johnson.

Marais was as quick as he could be, and copied down two telephone numbers and a home address before checking in the other book kept near the entrance. Shirley had been in the club on Saturday night.

"Any good fascist reason why I shouldn't stay on awhile and get through some blues, Sarge?"

"Not my piano," said Marais, pleased at how his English had improved in such company to include repartee.

Big Ben Goldstein looked like Nero after the fire insurance paid out. His clothes were the most expensive, his manicure came at fifty cents a cuticle, and his expression was one of ill-concealed glee.

Which misled some people into thinking he was not totally honest—not only the dishonest themselves, but others with old-fashioned prejudices. Ben was so honest that sometimes it hurt, but it hardly hurt at all to tell Trudy Stevenson there was nothing he could do for her that would be of help.

"And so, my love, we leave it there—all right? Don't worry, I'll not send a bill. If it'd just been Monty, then you had grounds. But I can't act now knowing what I do. You follow?"

"He's dead, and he was the only other one who knew! What can *they* prove?"

"Me, I wouldn't try them."

"You tricked me!"

"Okay, okay, so I tricked you. Better I should trick you than it happens in front of a judge. If the police are willing to drop everything now, so be it. Come back in the morning if you still want to discuss details so soon, the winding-up, all that. But I myself would see a doctor, get some pills. Elspeth, my dear, will you show this lady out?"

Mrs. Stevenson jerked her elbow free.

"You *bastard*," she hissed at Ben.

"Paternity suits I don't contest, madam."

"Wow!" said the delectable Elspeth, who had been left standing. "That was like a cork out of a bottle!"

The outer door slammed.

"No, that was Mrs. Rat out of a rat trap," Ben said sadly, and then started to dial the CID number. He owed it to the hard-arsed bugger to thank him for the warning.

"Only if it's pertinent to the matter in hand," warned the colonel as Kramer came back into the office. "Then we'll just have to start without Strydom."

Kramer sat down and said flatly, "I was right. We didn't crack Stevenson—the wife did."

"Hey?" exclaimed Marais, in great surprise. "What the hell gave you that idea, sir?"

"Sergeant, if I blasted you in the bum with a twelve-bore, could you tell me which pellet hit first?"

Crushed, Marais put his head back in the morning paper.

"Maybe it's time we all cooled down a bit," the colonel suggested after a while. "We'll give the DS two more minutes. Well, Tromp?"

"Sir?"

"Wouldn't Sergeant Marais at least hear a bang first?"

"*Ach,* I suppose it was the writing."

"Ja?"

"The assumption was that the suicide note ended with the man's initials, M.S. But the pencil line there was thin, so the pencil had to be sharp. So I read it again like it was what he first wrote—'Why not ask Shirley . . . ?'—and saw it was like a message he wanted passed on to me. 'Too late' could have been a reference to the time of night—you had used the word 'late' yourself, Colonel. He was in a hurry with an idea, but in writing it down this crystallized his position. Okay?"

"You're saying the suicide was on the other side only?" the colonel asked.

"Uh-huh. Look how neat and determined it is—a man who has complete control of himself because at last he knows just what to do. Hell, you need that frame of mind to do what he did. With the socks."

"But why no sign-off at the bottom?"

"No need. You expected me to take this personally, Colonel, and why? Because the tone is very personal, I agree. But did Marais or me give him *orders* to do anything? Christ, no. His appearance for remand was just a bloody *fact*—and Sam was supposed to get that through to him. And what do we, barbarians like us, care if he's only sorry for Jeremy? By that reckoning, we couldn't give a stuff. She didn't require any signature. Simple."

"And the pellets?" asked Marais, poised to begin a list.

"Oh, Jesus. Business so bad that 'every penny counts' and he pulls a stunt like this one, and yet his kid goes to riding lessons. The big come-down the wife made after she was sure she wasn't involved in the inquiries. The way she tried to make sure she did all the talking while we were at the house. His fluster over the sweet machine because they

108

hadn't been able to prepare the idea quick enough in the bedroom when she was doing her so-called checking. She wasn't expecting trouble—remember the crack about the Mormons? But she ad-libbed and it wasn't bad. And him blushing and sweating and we thought he was trying to cover for himself! And then I rang the reporter on the *Gazette* and asked him to see when that gymkhana was held."

"The one on their gate?" Marais asked.

"Uh-huh. That gymkhana was last Sunday. In other words, Ma Stevenson wasn't going to let anything get between little Jeremy and his moment of glory."

"But this is hypothesis, man," the colonel objected. "Or are you sure? Is this from Sam or something?"

"What I got from Sam was just a confirmation. You know him, sir; *you* try to break his bloody ethics. First I did ring him and what I learned was that Stevenson was a henpecked runt and that she really ran everything from the home, using the phone and expecting him to report any problems. No ethics in that—common hearsay, so I find out. I warn him to go easy. He rings back, says I did him a favor, and then a real shyster comes through wanting to slap charges on me. Seems Ma Stevenson is in his place, shouting for justice. So I tell him, too, and he—"

"And that was the last phone call? But what exactly was his story?"

"As soon as Stevenson found the body, he naturally rang her. She said leave everything and come home because she has to think this one over carefully. And when you think about it, that was more a female's reaction to a dead popsy with boobs like that. A bloke on his own would see Eve—"

"Ja, ja, as a terrible waste; I know. One thing more: do I take it these legal proceedings against us are now being reconsidered?"

Kramer nodded, and then the colonel announced they would wait until the quarter hour for Dr. Strydom to fight his way out of the jungle.

Constable Hein Wessels was so good at his job that if he'd tried free-lancing in another town he would have been arrested.

He stood on the corner of Monument and Claasens Streets, at the top end of Trekkersburg, looking like a waiting-room ashtray. And in unbelievable contrast, he pondered contentedly, to the trim figure, glowing with inner and outer cleanliness, that he had presented on the parade ground six months earlier. On the morning, for example, when he had been asked to forsake appearing in the graduation parade, and to grow his hair hideously long instead.

Now his double life was drawing to an end, but it had been good while it had lasted. As the Bible said somewhere, the better you were, the shorter time you stayed. A number of successful raids by the Drugs Squad, each initiated by his gift for timing, had begun to make things more difficult and, in some quarters, his stranger's face had begun to ring a bell. Soon it would be back into uniform for him, and the bottom rung to climb. Well, perhaps not quite the very bottom one, because his work had won him praise from above.

Plus warnings from those who had passed on, and who claimed to know the dangers as well as pleasures of belonging to an elite—or thinking you did. They would, for instance, occasionally remind him that he carried no firearm, and ask him to consider why this was true of no other white policeman. But that, surely, was a form of eliteness in itself, Wessels felt.

His mind wandered into arguments like these when there wasn't anything specific happening. Right then he was just keeping an eye on a yellow car with two black males in it, parked forty yards down Monument Street beside an empty plot and opposite a row of run-down shops, most of which were closed anyway. These blacks weren't doing anything, simply sitting there, and it was an area with a real mix-up of races during the day, being so near the station.

But Wessels was no fool. He tried to read the mud-splashed registration plate, and then shuffled, hawking and spitting, a little closer. This could easily be a new *dagga* drop-off point. And being Hein Wessels, you just never knew your luck; he might even try and approach them.

Marais put down the telephone and said, "Not at the mortuary, the hospital, or the prison."

"And who was that on the other line?" asked Kramer.

"Shirley's office. They say he's out and they don't know where to contact him; they're leaving a message. He's an interior designer, whatever that means."

"I don't think, gentlemen," said the colonel, "that Mr. Shirley will have anything very useful to add, or Stevenson would have thought of him much earlier. His final statement is accepted."

That had a ring to it that Kramer accorded a gracious nod. Marais nodded, too, vigorously.

"Furthermore, gentlemen, through an inquiry I myself arranged this morning, the night watchman at the shoe shop by the entrance to the alley states under oath that Stevenson, a known figure to him, went home as the city hall clock was chiming twelve-thirty. He keeps awake by listening for it, he says."

"Hey, that's a help," said Marais, then blushed.

"You have not spoken out of turn, Sergeant, so at ease, man. It *is* a big help. This watchman further states that nobody left the alley from twelve-thirty onwards."

"What about before then?" asked Kramer.

"Ah, there you spot the weakness. He did his last patrol inside the premises from midnight and reached the pavement only as the clock struck. He remained there until morning."

Kramer lit a Lucky and waited for the colonel to find his place again among Marais's notes. God, every conference was the same.

"Right, gentlemen. Miss Bergstroom was last seen alive at midnight and last heard alive slightly before twenty past. Between then and twenty-five past, when she was found by the manager, she had died."

"And an unidentified male was with her at the time," Kramer said, unchivalrously cutting across the preamble to steal the colonel's punch line.

"Oh, ja? So you've been doing some thinking, too?"

"Sorry, sir, but it made a difference having it all written down here, and the time to read it."

Marais put the newspaper down.

"Then you take it from there," the colonel said petulantly.

Then broke the silence by himself carrying on. "From the evidence before us, it would appear that a male was present. Warrant Gardiner reports that the drinking vessels had been cleaned of any prints, and the wash basin—which is only one reason I want the DS here—had been given a thorough rub-over. Which means, why should any guest— *Ach,* no; let's do this another way."

Kramer kept his eyes on the tip of his cigarette.

"This male is with Bergstroom," said the colonel, "and she gets killed by the snake. It's a private show maybe. Who knows? Anyhow, she is dead and because he's high-class—and here we have a fancy button to support that—this gives rise to social fears. He does not want it known that he was in the room of such a person, and at such a time as will cause him embarrassment following the publication of the inquest proceedings."

"Uh-huh."

"So he attempts to disguise his presence there. He cleans the glasses, but overlooks in his hurry—he had only seconds—that he put them down in the jam, which the girl would never do. He then wipes over the basin. The place is in such a hell of a mess, he doesn't notice the button."

"Or it isn't his," said Kramer unhelpfully.

"If Stevenson approaches at this time, there is nobody in the second dressing room, so he can hide there," the colonel said, not liking being interrupted. "Or he can get out before that, and just pull the front door closed behind him. He faces no real problems."

"I don't know, sir. It could have been more than a social fear, as you call it. Who takes prints after an accident?"

The colonel began to fiddle with the pieces of his broken ruler. "Go on, Tromp."

"Well, there is that chance, because the posters outside all said how dangerous it was, and because what happened seemed so—"

"Strydom?" the colonel said.

"One or two little slips in the past, although his examination of the body *in situ* was thorough, and I saw enough of the P.M. to realize that any bruises on the neck could only have been made by—"

"And you think . . . ?"

"He's been paying too much attention to the bloody snake from the beginning."

"But I want that snake to get attention, Tromp. I want every detail of the case looked over. I want all the staff interviewed for statements. I want semen from today's deceased, too, while we're on the subject. Enough has come to light now to change our whole attitude to the—"

"What about other causes?" Kramer asked. "That blow to

the back of the head—was it proved to be from her falling?"

"And poison?" Marais suggested. "I mean, the glasses were cleaned and—"

"*Ach*, no, Marais. He'd be bloody mad to leave them, and that would involve premeditation."

"Mulberry bushes, Kramer, mulberry bushes."

"You reject the idea of a blow, sir?"

"Not altogether, but I want everything gone over first. The snake marks are what worry me, in this respect."

"Why not after it was in its own death throes? Put there to fool us? He probably hit it on the head before touching it."

"The murderer, you mean?"

Kramer saw the broken edges of the ruler fitted together in a conscious gesture that made his eyes meet the colonel's and hold their gaze steadily.

It was left to Marais to notice Strydom listening and gloating in the doorway.

9

A space had been cleared on the colonel's desk, and shortly afterward an attendant from the museum arrived and placed on it a large enamel tray covered with a variety of colorful bits and pieces.

"But it's the most disgusting thing I've ever heard of," the colonel said, recoiling at the snake stink of ammonia. "You can't even imagine someone doing a thing like that!"

"The beauty of it," murmured Kramer, moving in to watch the demonstration.

"In the heat of the moment, Tromp?"

"Could've been, sir—or the bugger knew his snakes."

"You wanted to see, so I'm showing you," said Strydom.

"And I can assure you the facts speak for themselves," added Bose.

It was difficult at times to work out which of them was playing the straight man.

"What happened was that Mr. Bose here said the deceased must have had very strong arms to effect a break in the spinal cord," said Strydom. "And I had to explain to him that she was of slight to medium build, and that her hands had been found in place toward the ends of the reptile. We then discovered—"

"By empirical means," Bose interposed.

"Ja, by trying it ourselves with a bit of rope, we found that once you were holding a snake the same length by each end, you didn't have much power in your arms."

"The critical moment being when your arms begin to make an obtuse angle at the elbow and the leverage factor diminishes," Bose further explained. "Hence the difficulty of using a pair of chest expanders to their full width."

"Ta," said the colonel, who was good with the general public.

"But for safety reasons she'd keep holding the ends?" asked Kramer.

"Quite," agreed Bose. "She had to control both head and tail in an effort to—"

"Then we found slight tissue damage where her hands had gripped the python," went on Strydom, "not so much at the tail end, where the pressure was with the run of the scales, but certainly behind the head, once we'd wiped away surplus bleeding."

"And considerable damage at two other points much closer to the central loop of the body—and here we refer you to this section from the right lung, which shows severe bruising and even signs of having been torn."

"This is the liver, also showing contusion," said Strydom.

"And note, if you will," said Bose, "the deplorable state of the esophagus."

Marais tut-tutted.

"And a lot of force was used?" the colonel asked.

"A very considerable degree of it," Strydom replied, "as we established with the help of another snake when it had thawed—that's what took us so long. Man, you had to really hammer that thing to get the same amount of damage, squeeze till your whole bloody arm shook. Either the killer was a big bloke, or he was half out of his mind at the time— like when you don't know your own strength."

"That's a point," said Kramer. "He couldn't have been just trying to pull it off her?"

"*Ach*, what about the other evidence, Tromp?"

"I don't know about that," said Strydom, "but do you try and get a tie off by pulling hard on either side? Never! And besides, he was pulling it this way because, as we said before, the spinal—"

"We'd also like to draw your attention to this sample of skin taken from a point where severe bruising occurred."

"Ja, Mr. Bose?"

"You'll observe that the fingertips dug in very deeply."

"And if that had been the deceased, then her nails—which were long and pointy—would have gone right through," Strydom declared triumphantly, looking around.

Then Bose slipped out of the room, called the attendant to remove the tray, and made his own quiet farewell.

"Let's go," said Kramer.

While nine blocks to the east, a yellow car drew away and turned into Claasens Street.

Wessels, hidden in the narrow entrance to a derelict barber-shop, shrugged. He could not win them all. It had just occurred to him that a pickup might have been timed to take place around the corner, when he found himself boxed in by a swaying figure.

"Morning, my baasie! Is my baasie enjoying the sunshine?"

It was the colored pusher Rex du Plooi, already with the staggers at that hour, and holding up an empty bottle to his ear as if listening for the sea. Many whites believed coloreds were a mixture of the worst characteristics of all the races whose blood ran in their veins; more often than not, Wessels had discovered, this was gross slander. But in Rex's case it seemed true, and it needed only some cheap wine to turn him into a Molotov cocktail that might, at any moment, explode.

"Ja, you've got it in one, Rex—enjoying the sunshine."

"That's nice, my baasie, that's wonderful, I say."

He must have had a profitable night, and some devious questioning, Wessels knew, could have its rewards. But one foot wrongly placed, with Rex in that condition, could be a foot in one or the other's grave.

Fear fizzled pleasantly inside him, heightening his perception.

"Seems like you've been on a *lekker* trip also—hey, Rex?"

"My baasie?"

"I just said things looked good with you."

"But how are things with *you,* my baasie?"

"Told you, man."

"Only there is no sunshine this side, you see? That's why I am worried to find you in this cold, dirty place with dog *kak* and frikkies on the floor."

Wessels glanced down. He hadn't noticed the used condoms and excrement, and had even stood in some of it.

"Sunshine's in a guy's head, Rex—you should know that."

"But those are big eyes you've got, my baasie."

"Why's that?"

But Wessels thought he knew the answer already: he had stuck his nose a little too obviously right into one of Rex's own drop-offs—and it was not only a delaying tactic the pusher had in mind. So he did not hesitate before jabbing a thumb into each of the other's big eyes and taking to his heels.

Jesus, that was his cover blown once and for all, but there was still the chance of a final feather in his cap.

He ran round into Claasens Street and dodged a meager flow of pedestrians until he caught sight of the yellow car double-parked across the other side.

But now there was only the driver in it.

A driver whose vigilant attitude confirmed suspicion beyond a doubt: the passenger was out making the drop at that very moment. The all-important thing was to see from which alleyway or building he emerged, and to get another look at that registration number.

Wessels kept to his side of the street, but moved in as close as he dared without giving himself away, and hid behind the wired-in back of a parked truck. Again he was in luck, for the sun's rays were now striking at an angle that made the numerals, punched in relief on the rear plate, visible despite the mud. He had read off 4544 when there was a sharp honk and he looked up to see the driver's hand return to the wheel. The bugger was getting jumpy.

Then not even a backfire could distract Wessels as he concentrated on identifying the district letters that prefixed the number. It seemed to be Trekkersburg's, but he had to be sure. It was: NTK.

"Bloody hell!" said Wessels. In the three seconds it had taken him to do that, the passenger was back in the car and was being driven off at high speed in the direction of Peacevale. In his opinion, he had just seen the impossible.

But he was given no time to dwell on it. Just then, over on the other side of the street, someone started yelling "Police!" and he jogged across to see what the fuss was about.

News of a raid on the Munchausen Café reached Kramer as he was rounding off Marais's briefing.

"Just hang on a sec. Now, Sergeant, you've got that? A list of everyone who was in the club that night and check every alibi. The ones who split from their party or sat alone, anything like that, I want you to give the works to. Okay, Zondi, what's your case?"

Zondi told him what he knew. It was garbled but enough.

Then Zondi moved them nine blocks east through rush-hour traffic in under two minutes. The Chev was left to take care of itself once they entered Claasens Street, now a traffic jam, and the crowd outside the café had two holes barged through it.

"Jesus Christ," said Kramer.

Through the wide doorway he could see Wessels, Constables Smit and Hamlyn in uniform, and an old woman kneeling over a body, while a tall foreigner looked on.

"That's more than just shooting, boss," Zondi murmured with a nod.

"Eyewitnesses," said Kramer.

"Right," said Zondi, and turned to the crowd.

As Kramer entered the café Wessels came up and gave a concise account of what he had seen and heard, adding that the victim was breathing his last, following a bullet wound in the head.

"Uh-huh. Tell Smit to get outside and clear a path for Kloppers and the doc. Hamlyn better stand on the door."

"And me, sir?"

"What about that car number?"

"I've given it to Control, sir."

"Good. *Ach,* start on interviewing the nonwhite staff—how many?"

"Just that cook and a waiter."

"Then while it's still fresh, hey? You know how fast these kinds of memories can dwindle."

Kramer sat down at a table near the window, took a straw from the glass of them on the checked tablecloth, and looked round the room. It was nothing special. A typical café. A typical café whether run by Indians, Greeks, Italians, or Portuguese. Yellow walls, blue floor tiles, wooden tables, chairs made out of chromed pipe, big electric fans, pictures of sunsets and snow-capped mountains, a jukebox, menus in plastic stands, all as plain and simple as its fare, made inviting by the aroma of hot dogs and soup. When the man died, that's when it would look different.

The general impression would go, and in its place would come tedious exact measurements, notes on its little oddities and exclusive features, photographs by the bucketful, and a

118

requirement that all this should reconcile with what could have happened. Had happened.

The tableau about the body changed. The old woman sat back on her thin heels, and the foreigner crossed himself.

What made the Munchausen look different from many other cafés was the mezzanine floor, or balcony, above Kramer's head, which brought the ceiling down to a much cozier height. Or what would have seemed cozier if its structure had not been so flimsy and doubtful. He would check what was up there. Then again, there was not much of a counter, and that stuck away in the far corner with the till on it, and glass cases of cigarettes behind it. On the near side of the till was a rack festooned with cellophane packets containing potato chips, biltong, dried beef sticks, and other goodies. The rack could well obscure a view of the doorway. He would check on that first.

Skirting the dead man and mourners, Kramer went and placed himself behind the open till. Visibility was good. He then noticed that the kitchen door could also be seen from this position, off to his right, and assumed that the manager liked to keep an eye on both his customers and his staff without having to move about much.

The balcony, he noted, was reached by a single flight of wooden stairs screened off against the outer wall. The left-hand third appeared to be a small office, and the rest had three more tables to offer. Yet plainly for a better class of meal, as he could make out napkins folded like bishops' hats, and the décor included fishing nets, big glass balls, and old wine bottles with straw around them.

He looked again at the street.

Wessels came out of the kitchen and wandered over.

"The chef was doing lunches for boys to fetch for their bosses, the waiter was helping him, and Mrs. Funchal—that's the old lady—was whipping up something special. I was wrong, sir; there's also a black dishwasher who is down at the clinic getting a tooth out."

"But what did they see?"

"Nothing. Heard the bang and Mrs. Funchal told the chef to see what was going on—it didn't register with any of them it was a gun—and he stuck his head out. Nobody was in the café. Then he put his head out further and looked this way to see if Mr. Funchal—that's the old woman's son—knew what

119

it was about. He saw the till open and then Mr. Funchal's hand. They dragged him out onto the floor there."

"What about him?" said Kramer, nodding at the man still standing beside the body.

"That's Da Gama, their nephew. He was yelling 'Police' when I ran in. He'd been up on the balcony, working in the office. He also thought it was a backfire and didn't come down immediately. His aunt's scream brought him."

"She was screaming for you first, then?"

"That's right, sir. I wasn't in time to stop them moving him, but that's where he was."

And Wessels pointed just to the left of where Kramer was standing.

"So, man, where did the bullet hit?"

"Smack between the eyes, sir. He's not as tall as you, and I reckon that the killer fired it from his own shoulder height straight across the counter because otherwise it would've gone through this stuff and I can't find any holes."

Wessels demonstrated what he meant, holding an imaginary firearm at right angles to the counter between the till and the rack.

"Looks like it, but we'd better wait for Doc Strydom's little words of wisdom."

"Hell, the bastard was fast, sir!"

"Ja, so I've heard. How much was taken?"

But just then the tall man approached, very shaken, and shyly took off his hat. He surprised Kramer by having very blond hair while otherwise conforming to type—not the squat and jolly one, as the dead man appeared to have been, but its twin, the thin and miserable one. His eyes had the hardness of a man well acquainted with suffering.

"That is my uncle," he said.

"Mr. Da Gama?"

"Mario Da Gama. Are you the police chief?"

"Lieutenant Kramer, Murder and Robbery."

"That what it was," Da Gama said bitterly.

"Know how much is missing?"

Da Gama went over to the till.

"Don't touch!" Kramer warned.

"Phew! Eighty—one hundred? I must check in my cash-book. It was little." And he shook his head.

"Looks like someone's arrived, sir," said Wessels. "Oh,

120

must be relatives that have got the news."

"I ring them," said Da Gama. "They come to take Mama away. Would you like me to look in the book now?"

"Fine, on my way. Wessels, go and tell Smit he can let two women in, but they must take the old lady and get out again, hey?"

"Sir."

"No trouble. I fetch the book," Da Gama offered.

"Less trouble if I come," replied Kramer, eager to quit the ground floor before an emotional scene began.

And he followed Da Gama up the staircase onto the balcony, feeling he had gone up on deck, for a strong breeze was buffeting in through little windows that were open over the street.

"Smell of the cheap food," explained Da Gama, noticing his raised brow. "The hamburger, you know? It all comes up here and can spoil the work of many hours. This place is for the specialty customers."

"Oh, ja?"

"The special dishes of the house that Mama makes. I serve them myself sometime. Only at night, you understand?"

"Very nice."

"Oh, I must have the roll from the till, Chief. How can I take if I don't touch? Just one button I must press."

"Okay, you get it then," Kramer said, disenchanted with tills as a source of incriminating fingerprints.

But thought he had better see that Da Gama didn't paw everything, so he went over to the balcony railing. The thing extended farther than he had realized and, without actually leaning over it, all he could see was the counter and a bit of unoccupied floor. He was grateful for these limitations, as the sound of the old woman being dragged away was quite enough.

He concentrated instead on the crown of Da Gama's curious blond mop, and on where the man was putting his hands, but it seemed all proper care was taken.

"Well, how does it look?" he asked, when the record of the morning's business arrived.

"Not a good day, Chief. Twenty-one rand—plus float. Come inside."

They went into the small office, which was stacked with old invoices and other stuff that should have been thrown away years before. Their weight made the thin floor seem even more likely to give suddenly.

Da Gama started small avalanches on the cluttered desk in his efforts to find the cashbook, and hurt himself when he slapped a hand down to prevent a wad of slips on a wire spike from falling, too.

Kramer sat astride the larger of the two chairs and waited, looking around at the pictures of bleeding hearts and bloody lambs, and wondering what the water in the dish screwed near the door would taste like.

"Eighty-seven rand, maybe fifty cents," said Da Gama, circling his grand total on the back of the telephone directory.

Kramer could not help a short laugh. That was peanuts. The crazy bastards had done it again.

Marais had been charmed by Shirley's manner.

Usually an accent like that set his right foot on edge and not, he thought, without reason. Once, as a very new man on the beat, he had responded to a break-in report at a big posh house, only to be told the occupiers weren't going to be disturbed twice in one night, and he'd jolly well better come back in the morning. Some people . . .

But Shirley had been quite the opposite on the phone: polite, friendly, and very happy to be of assistance with routine inquiries, although he could not imagine how. The only snag had been finding a suitable time to meet, as he already had a number of unbreakable engagements planned for the afternoon. Then they had hit upon the idea of making it a date for four-thirty, when Shirley would be popping home to do a quick change before cocktails at Justice Green-hill's—yes, of the Supreme Court, the very same.

So, feeling far less daunted now by the thought of having to mix in Trekkersburg high society, Marais decided to pay surprise visits on the rest of his list; the post office had been very helpful in giving him addresses to match the business numbers he had collected.

If they were all like that, he could not go wrong.

Da Gama, now apparently maudlin with grief, was insisting on telling Kramer his whole life story—or something like it. Kramer was not really listening, but intent on what Strydom might be able to tell him when the examination was finished.

What he did gather was that Uncle José, apart from being a lovable old eccentric who owned nine tearooms and still felt a need to work in the most humble, had lived in South Africa practically all his life. In contrast, pathetically painted, to Da Gama, who had wasted his years in Moçambique before being driven out. In fact, if it hadn't been for Uncle José, who had no sons of his own, and whose daughters were all nuns, Da Gama would not have known where to turn. But the old man had taken him to his heart, had put clothes on his back, and had even found a little job for him. Truly the man was a saint.

"Uh-huh," said Kramer, thinking the old bugger had at least made a start in the right direction.

"So what happens now, Chief?"

"You show one of my men how you want the place locked up, and then you'd better get along to the family."

"It is not our custom," mumbled Da Gama, turning his hat around in his hands by the brim. "Also the priest is coming. I must wait for him."

"Then wait in your office, okay? Sorry, but this officer here has got pictures to take, and you'll be in his way."

"Okay," said Da Gama, and went upstairs.

"How's it?" asked Gardiner, stopping by while he changed lenses.

"How do you think, man?"

"I heard Wessels maybe had an ident on one of them."

"Ja, but he says they were in heavy shade all the time. Still, I've sent him back to CID to look through the books."

"And Zondi?"

"Zero."

"So we go through the motions," said Gardiner, and wandered off behind the counter to take a wide shot.

But Kramer refused to succumb to the shoulder-sagging apathy that had begun to pervade the place. Perhaps a proper look at the corpse might restore a sense of purpose.

He walked over briskly and stood beside Strydom, careful not to get in his light.

José Funchal had a hole where his thick eyebrows met that looked like a jab made with a red-hot poker. After that you noticed the deeply bruised eyelids, the cigarette burn on the broad upper lip, and the stubble on the bull-mastiff cheek.

He wore a gold signet ring, bearing the same design as the one Da Gama had, and no other jewelry. His clothes were freshly laundered, but obviously bought at a bazaar. Which all fitted the legend.

"Losing faith in me?" asked Strydom.

"Always."

"It's the twenty-two again."

"Uh-huh. Nice neat hole, hey? Perfect round shape."

"The bullet must have struck at right angles almost precisely, level with the ground, which may give you some idea of the assailant's height. The shot must have been fired sighting on the eye."

"Same again then, Doc? Around five-eight?"

"Ja, that should narrow things down by a few million," said Strydom, closing his notebook and pointing with his pen to the area around the wound.

"No tattoos from powder, no smoke marks. Range the usual three feet to thirty."

"Say four, with the counter taking up two of them."

"Say what you like, Tromp, but this isn't how we're going to catch them."

Strydom stood up and made a face to convey his apologies for that remark.

"True, but it just shows what cold-blooded bastards they are. No warning, no struggle—just bam. And another thing I don't get: they're damn crack with their guns. Where did they practice?"

"Now you're just trying to add to your problems."

"No, I mean it."

They moved over to a table and sat down, waiting for Kloppers to arrive. Strydom began to thumb through his notebook.

"What you really mean is they fire one shot and they're away."

"They have to, for the speed," said Kramer.

"Ja, but in the matter of accuracy, take the butcher, for instance: that twenty-two was fired inches from him and went in at an angle. In Lucky's case, they hit him as he was turning away, and the thirty-eight traveled just inside the skull up the left-hand side. Only one of the others came near to being a fluke like this one, and then it wasn't nearly as good."

124

"Uh-huh? And what's a fluke? Getting something right and then letting it become a matter of opinion?"

Strydom laughed and threw down the paper napkin he had been fiddling with.

"Okay, you win on words," he said. "But in practical terms, could you guarantee the same result with a twenty-two in your hand—even four feet away?"

Kramer shook his head.

"But tell me, Tromp, there is something behind this nonsense of yours. What is it?"

Kloppers had clumped in with his metal tray before the right reply had been found—or something close to it.

"Doc, if crime was a sport, what would these buggers be? Champions?"

"Too true!"

"And what does a boxing champ do before his first big fight?"

"I see! He works his way up on small purses."

"*Ach*, no. He gets himself some bloody sparring partners and works on his weaknesses. You think about it."

Strydom had not moved much when Kramer glanced back at him through the café window.

10

But the colonel found Kramer's notion fanciful, and suggested some good sense of his own.

"Now listen, Tromp, you know how their mind works. If a man is white, then he is automatically rich. It doesn't matter whether you and me can see he couldn't find two cents to pay the rent with; as far as they are concerned, white is the color of money."

"True," Kramer conceded, flicking his match into the CID courtyard below. "But that's with your petty criminal."

"And what are these? Okay, so they can shoot, and they can drive, and they can run bloody fast, but what else can you say about them? They're bloody stupid, like all the rest. I tell you what did me good today: I had lunch with the brigadier and we discussed this matter. 'Hans,' he says to me, 'what do you blokes think you're doing? Just stop a moment and see this in its true perspective. Tell me how many cases of armed robbery on small businesses you've dealt with, and how many times you found one eyewitness to help solve who did it.' Then I had to admit that in all my years it was only twice, and both times a European came forward. All the other times we acted on information received once the bastards started spending their money or getting drunk and boasting in the shebeens. 'That's how it is with robbery investigation,' the brigadier said, and I tell you that made me feel a fool."

"In other words, sir?"

"With murder, you look for a motive," the colonel said, his tone becoming circumspect, "but with robbery, it is staring you in the face. They want money, so they kill and rob for it —every day, all over the country. Life? Life matters nothing to them. Yet now you start trying to read something new into this, as if it was a specific case where you were asking, Why kill this man?"

Kramer watched a bird fly up from the single rosebush to peck at the fruit on the palm tree. His cigarette grew a long ash, unheeded.

"Hell, is there some personal involvement I don't know about?" the colonel said, laughing softly and nudging him in the side. But his eyes gleamed shrewdly.

"I drop this for the Bergstroom case until someone starts talking?"

"Never. People are at risk with these lunatics round—don't get me wrong. Marais can carry on with the routine meantime. It seems a hard thing to say, but that was only a one-off when we come to choosing priorities. Plus I've got doubts now about that snake thing. Old Stry—"

"Two, if you count Stevenson."

"Man, you're quibbling, hey? You're still thinking too much. Let's have some action. Tell Zondi to get his finger out and try and get something from the other side; that's our only chance. And see you chase him."

"And who's going to chase Marais?"

"Not me," said the colonel, walking off to his office.

It hadn't been bad sense after all.

Wessels was waiting for Kramer with a photograph in his hand, taken from one of the books he had been told to go through.

"I've got a possible here, sir," he said eagerly.

"Who's he when he's at home?"

"Gosh Twala, Bantu male, aged forty-three."

"Never heard of him. Come."

They went the length of the corridor and into Kramer's office. Zondi had his feet comfortably arranged up against the filing cabinet.

"Hey! Wake up, you! Gosh Twala—know him?"

"Small time, boss."

"Doing what?"

"Stealing cars, got eight years in sixty-six for it—Sithole's case."

"And recently?"

"Last I know of him, he was working at the brickworks."

"That *skabengas'* paradise! But that means he's pretty washed up, then, in with the hard-case assaults and the rest."

Zondi nodded, and said, "Terrible work, that, many men getting hit with the blow back. But the trouble with Twala is that he tells Sithole who buys the cars from him and he took three others inside. Now nobody will buy from him; he is finished."

"Yet I'm almost sure it's the same one as was driving the car," said Wessels. "Had a longer look at him than the other, and there's the same flatness to the back of the head, and the ears that stick out."

"Well, Zondi? Worth picking him up?"

"He is a good driver, and has got many licenses."

"Need help?"

Zondi shook his head, flipped his hat onto it, and sauntered out.

"What do I do now, sir?" asked Wessels, as Kramer flopped back in his chair and stared at the wall.

"I think it's time you took that wig off and put on some clothes."

"Sir?"

"You're the nearest we've got to an eyewitness, so I've fixed with the colonel for you to be transferred to us meantime. Okay?"

"Fine, sir!"

"Then report back in one hour. Go."

As Wessels sped from the room, the telephone rang. Kramer ignored it for a while and then lifted the receiver. A yellow Ford, NTK 4544, had been found abandoned not a quarter of a mile from the café, and Fingerprints were investigating.

The lanes dividing the block behind the courthouse had once been what Marais liked best about Trekkersburg, if he had to like anything. They were like the windbreaks in a plantation, zigzagging here and there and crisscrossing, all without any apparent plan, yet leaving you sure there was one. While the plaster twirly-whirlies and pillars and hanging signs with fancy lettering, creaking on their brackets, made you think you were in a Three Musketeers film.

But he had had a gutsful of superior bastards, and they had spoiled everything for him. They had spoiled his morning, his toasted cheese sandwich, and now they had done damage to his afternoon.

There was nothing romantic about the lanes any longer; they were just grubby passageways between offices with empty, forbidding hallways, and shops that sold cracked vases and dirty spoons kept in glass cases; while the odd glimpse of a haughty typist painting her nails was about as off-putting as the unpleasant smell of duplicating ink.

He stopped for a moment to watch an old black crone flattening out a cardboard carton she had taken from a stack of refuse awaiting removal. She stamped on it, crawled on it, and then added it to a pile already so big she would never lift it. The pile shifted and he saw she had a homemade wheelbarrow underneath. It was true what they said: some of them were beginning to use brains instead of backsides.

Marais was stalling, although he would not admit it. He was trying to delay his entrance into the hallway of number 22, right opposite, by wondering if the crone was committing an offense, and then drifting into the dizzying legalities of how you established the ownership of rubbish between its disposal and its collection. No good; he would just have to get on with the job and have done with it.

"Whoa—where do you think you're going?" a voice boomed out behind him, making him slide on the coconut matting.

It was Goldstein the lawyer, shouting down at him from his second-floor office on the other side.

"I'm making inquiries," Marais replied stiffly.

"What, in his place? My boy, you don't know the *trouble* you're making! From two to four, my friend there is in special consultation."

"That's not my worry."

"Tell me you're joking! Tell me your heart is not so hardened against the world! Would you tear a man from the very bosom of his personal—"

"Oh, do bugger off, Ben!" another voice called out, from somewhere directly overhead.

Ben waved his cigar at whoever it was.

"Who is the little twit down there anyway?" the voice above asked lazily.

"Tomorrow in A Court I take you apart a piece at a time," Ben shouted across with massive mock confidence. "Don't be late, you hear?"

Then he puckered up, blew his unseen rival a kiss, and closed the window.

Marais, who had other fish to fry, walked straight out and never went back.

Beneath one of four towering chimney stacks, Zondi stood and waited impatiently. The brick dust was terrible; not only was the ground covered with it, but the air itself was gritty.

Then the foreman came out of his office, shaking one sandal to dislodge a stone caught between his fat pink toes, and beckoned to him.

"Next time you bring a chit with you, see?"

"The lieutenant said all right?"

"No, he bloody didn't. He wasn't there, but some other European knows you, so I suppose you can go ahead. It's just I'm not having any damn wog coming here thinking he can do what he likes and starting trouble with my boys. Twala? Was that the one?"

"Yes, please, sir. He is at work today?"

"How the hell am I supposed to know that? You ask his *induna*; he gives me the absentees list."

"Where do I find him?"

"The *induna*?"

"Yes, sir."

This delay was beginning to seriously worry Zondi. He had already felt long, sullen glares being made in his direction from the ragged men hand-pushing trucks of brick from the kilns. Many of them knew him, and soon the alert would have reached the farthest corner of the works.

"*Ach*, I'm not here to do your work for you. Ask that *keshla* over there," said the foreman, completing his scrutiny of Zondi's identity card and handing it back.

The old-timer was hardly any more cooperative. He pulled his torn jacket over the burn marks on his chest, which looked like splatters of tar, the scarring was so thick, and mumbled something about oven number 9.

"Have I asked a simple man a simple question?" Zondi snapped.

"Who do you seek?"

"Twala."

"*Hau!* He is a bad one—you must go carefully with him."

"Would you like to see that?"

130

The *keshla* grinned, showing he still had three teeth in the front, and began to lead the way, skipping nimbly on his bowed legs over the rubble of spoiled bricks.

They went under an overhead passageway and Zondi realized he was right beside the firing house itself, with the kiln entrances, round-topped and low, set in its curving wall at intervals of about twenty yards. The *keshla* explained that those that had been bricked up were awaiting the heat to give the bricks their hardness. The men sealing number 8 stopped work as Zondi approached and backed aside to allow him to pass, the cement sliding from their trowels unnoticed in their undisguised loathing for him. One face, hooded by a sack which was protecting the shoulders for carrying, turned quickly away—but not before Zondi had recognized a once notorious illicit liquor distiller, whom he had put behind bars and out of business. Truly, with all the fires and the dangers, the place was close to a hell itself, he thought soberly. Better to dig ditches all day in the sun.

An electric cable had been run into the kiln to provide lighting while the bricks were stacked, and Zondi followed it alone, the *keshla* suddenly losing his lust for witnessing the confrontation.

There was none. The *induna,* found dozing behind some completed work, swore that Twala had not turned up for work that morning, and called over his work team to verify this.

How entirely true this was, they all agreed, and said what a shame it was that the policeman had come so far and found nothing. And on second thought, the Twala he described to them didn't sound at all like the one they knew. Maybe he should try the aluminum factory or the car assembly plant.

In this they totally overdid it.

Zondi found his way out into the open again and looked around. Then he noticed that the entrance to number 8 was still short of its top six rows of bricks, and drew his pistol.

"Build," he said to the men.

Nobody moved.

He caught one of them with his left hand, spun him around and slammed him against the others.

"Build!" he shouted.

The kiln entrance was only five bricks wide, and took very

little time to fill in, with nobody paying much attention to the niceties.

A terrified Gosh Twala erupted through it not long after.

From the railway up, the hillsides were a deep, lush green, and very few homes were visible from the road, although Marais could see rooftops here and there behind the hedges and bamboo thickets. Hibiscus grew on the broad lawns, and hydrangeas, their huge pale clusters of flowers as good as white stones, marked the entrances to many of the driveways. For its part in the luxuriant scheme of things, the municipality had planted thick-flamed cannas on the road islands and center strips.

The other traffic was made up mainly of delivery vehicles from the best stores, liquor orders on motorcycles, and small English cars filled with dogs and children with pedigrees.

Except for the usual nannies, playing with their charges out on the lawns where they could talk with friends, there was nobody about.

Marais wished he had thought to bring a map. Then he saw a burglar alarms maintenance engineer in a van and stopped him for directions.

The number of the place was 34 and it had a name as well, Glenwilliam, in wrought iron on the gate. The drive was long, bending round to the right under enormous fig trees, and it was not until Marais topped a rise in the straight section that the double-story house came into view between the silver flash of birch trees.

Three vehicles stood in the doorless garage which had been burrowed into a high bank covered in desert plants. There was a white Jaguar, a plum Datsun coupe, and a conventional Land-Rover with a towing bar for the motorboat nearby, leaving one bay empty but with sump stains that suggested it had an occupant overnight. He looked at his watch: only four twenty-seven. Mr. Shirley couldn't be home yet, so he would wait a couple of minutes. Houses that size tended to belittle him.

Marais had hardly settled back when a middle-aged black girl came to rap at his window.

"The missus asks if the master wouldn't like to come inside, please," she said in a soft unafraid voice.

"Are you sure?"

"I have made tea specially for you coming. Do not be afraid of the dog. He only bites persons he does not know—never persons who I take into the house."

"Huh!" said Marais, not liking the way it growled deep in its wolfish chest, yet getting out before he remembered to check his hair in the rear-view. He did this in one of the car windows and then followed her across.

More servants should work in places like these and then there would be less complaining, he thought, amused by the fold of fat above each swinging elbow and by her waddle.

There were bulrushes on the wooden chest in the hall, and a mat that didn't stick too well to the highly polished floor.

The room he was shown into was also a disappointment: no oil paintings on its walls, no huge, soft armchairs and highwayman's pistols. Just some cane seats painted cream, one big table with flowers heaped on it, and some pots to arrange them in. The girl went out.

And her mistress entered a moment later, holding out a ringed hand with a straight arm. Her age baffled him: the wrinkled throat was like an old tree, but the face itself was as smooth as a wood carving—one that had been given a coat of almost pure white with no underseal, so it showed up gray in the incised lines down either side of the mouth.

"Oh, Martha has managed to coax you in. I'm so glad."

The handshake was a touch.

"I'm his mother."

"Pleased to meet you, Mrs. Shirley. You knew I was coming?"

"Peter phoned, wretched child, just as I was getting ready to go out to bridge. Insisted I should be here in case he might be a minute or two late."

"*Ach*, I'm sorry."

"Don't be ridiculous. One can't treat guests in a cavalier fashion. Although you're not quite a guest, are you?"

"Not exactly, but I don't think you could call it business either."

"I most certainly wouldn't have one of his clients here, and he has tried that one on, Mr. . . . ?"

"Sergeant Marais."

"What squad? I once met a colonel or something at a dinner—my husband is a retired judge, by the way."

"Murder and Robbery, madam."

133

"Do sit down, Sergeant. You're making me quite wilt at the sight of you."

Wilting was exactly what Marais felt he was doing; this was nothing like the reception he had imagined. Mrs. Shirley started to stick flowers onto the spikes in a round piece of lead.

"And this is all because of that horrid little man and his dreadful affairs? What on earth could he have done to her that we're being fed these gruesome stories about puff adders or whatever it was?"

"That's our job to find out," Marais said, seating himself on the edge of a chair that squeaked.

"But is it really necessary?" she asked, taking up garden scissors to snip the heads off some roses.

"The law must be upheld, Mrs. Shirley."

"Good heavens, you're trying to tell me what the law must or mustn't do? When I've been married to it thirty years? I meant is it really necessary, required of you, to hound Peter in this fashion?"

"Hey? I'm only doing what I was told—to get the accounts of movements by all members present in the club that night. Your son, Mr. Shirley, is just unfortunate that so far we haven't been able to contact anyone who saw him leave—or, in fact, verify what happened to him after midnight."

"Is that all?" Mrs. Shirley said testily.

"Sorry?"

"I'm sure Martha and I have distinct memories of his arrival home on Saturday night."

"Oh, ja?"

"Or are you solely interested in what he has to say?"

Marais rose slightly to look out the window. No other car had arrived yet.

"If it's not any trouble, I'll appreciate it," he said, taking out his notebook to reinforce this impression. "The more the merrier, as they say."

Her cold stare went in through his eyes and all the way down his back.

This simply wasn't his day somehow.

The door was locked and Zondi came to open it in his shirtsleeves, half smiling when he saw who it was.

"Any joy?" asked Kramer, entering the interrogation

room and taking a look at what stood against the wall.

Gosh Twala had changed a lot since his last picture, as if it had been taken by one of those swanky crooks in the main street and now the retouching had come off. His cheeks were hollowed and his eyes had no brightness in them, while his skin had that dull look, like a blackboard not wiped properly, which was a sure sign of a really poor coon.

"He swears he was not absent on the days in question and says the *induna* will swear to this also."

"Is that right, Twala?"

"*Hau*, yes, please, my master! True's God!"

"This *induna* I know to be a liar," Zondi said.

"So he could have been sneaking off?"

"It is possible."

But Kramer knew from the way Zondi said it that little interest or conviction went with it.

"Why bring him in?"

"There were difficulties, boss. The foreman is a very formal man."

"Oh, ja?"

"Also I want to know why he hides from me. He says it is because his name is being shouted at the office and the other boys tell him I am there."

"I am fright!" said Twala, raising hands like a beggar.

"Pockets?"

"Nothing."

"And of course he denies any knowledge of the robberies themselves?"

Zondi nodded.

"What about Constable Wessels? Has he seen him?"

Again Zondi nodded. The apathy was on its way again—still nothing positive. There had not been a single trace of a fingerprint or anything else in the yellow Ford.

"Have you made him do the jumps yet?"

"No boss," answered Zondi, and had Twala leap about so as to drop anything he might have secreted inside himself, a prison trick with tobacco readily adapted to hide *dagga* as well.

Then the door opened and Sithole said, "Excuse me, Lieutenant, but a car has been found."

"Ach, I know that, man," Kramer replied irritably, "so just bugger off."

135

He was watching a scarlet stain spreading in the filthy pullover Twala wore next to his skin.

"Did you do that, Zondi?"

"*Hau!* Let me look! This is a knife wound, boss."

"You're slipping, hey?"

Then Twala began protesting he'd only been trying to defend himself, and it had been the other fool's fault for drinking so much and he hadn't killed him anyway, just taught him a lesson. The rest was entirely in Zulu.

At the end of which Sithole again poked his head in and said, "Excuse me, Lieutenant, but this is a crashed car with persons in it."

Everything changed when Peter Shirley finally arrived home in his MG sports, most apologetic for having been half an hour late, but a couple of tasteless idiots had nearly driven him screwy by picking holes in a wall covering that was just perfect for them.

"Hardly a profession," Mrs. Shirley sniffed, accepting her son's peck on an uplifted cheek.

And then, to Marais's considerable relief, withdrew.

Shirley was not quite as imagined either. He and Marais shared a stocky, fairly average build, and then went their separate ways. His hair was three inches longer, his body was good but a little soft, and his eyes had seen nothing. Also, his fingernails were bitten right down. His mum should have put aloe juice on them, or mustard; that would have killed the habit before it was too late. Yet, for all that, he still seemed a nice bloke.

"It doesn't look as if you've had any of this tea," Shirley said to him as soon as they were alone.

"Well—er—we were just having a chat. Your mum—Mrs. Shirley was giving me an account of your movements."

"Great, but sorry you had to be stranded with the Dragon. Look, I'll just get Martha to do us another pot."

"But aren't you in a hurry?"

"Nothing deadly—and don't worry about Martha. She's a poppet."

Marais stood up and stretched, then inspected the flower arrangement, which was still unfinished, with all the long ones to one side instead of in the middle.

Shirley was gone only about two minutes, and then came

back in, stuffing an enormous wedge of chocolate cake into his mouth. He held out a plate for Marais to select a piece of his own.

"That's *lekker;* thanks, hey?"

"Martha again. Brilliant! Can do aboulutely anything. I've tried to interest her in improving her literacy, though, but she won't."

"The best ones know their place."

"There you and I might beg to differ," Shirley replied, smiling warmly, "but naturally you see a much seamier side of African community life than I do. Must tend to distort things a little."

"*Ach,* in my opinion, a kaffir is a kaffir—doesn't matter what side you look at."

Shirley laughed and choked on a cake crumb, patting himself hard on the back.

Then Martha brought in a fresh pot of tea and Marais made a point of thanking her for it in Sesotho, the only Bantu language he spoke. She giggled gratifyingly and wobbled off.

"I could speak Zulu as a kid," Shirley said, "but now I'm afraid it's all gone out of the window. Milk?"

"And three sugars, please."

"Pity the old man's away bundu-bashing. You two should get on famously; lots in common and all that."

Marais nodded, very flattered that here at least was someone who regarded him as good as the next man in the pursuit of justice. Then he swallowed his tea hurriedly so he could get his notebook out and cause no extra inconvenience.

Shirley leaned toward him attentively, his chin cupped in one hand, and said, "Well? What exactly can I help you with?"

"Just routine, you understand: your movements last Saturday night."

"God, what an evening! I had this little nurse lined up, positively aching to forget bedpans for a while, and she didn't appear."

"Should have asked us to find her," joked Marais.

"Must remember that next time! Blind date, to be honest; waited for her at the nurses' home and she didn't pitch up. Left a note, thinking she might have been kept late on the ward—often happens—and went on waiting at the Wigwam.

The usual crowd came in after a bit, but I wasn't in the mood, and sat at one of Monty's tables for two. I mean, she might have got a lift up at any minute, and I wasn't having one of them get his paws on her."

"You said Monty? You were on those sorts of terms?"

"Did his place for him; twenty percent discount and a free membership for life—oh, that wasn't clever, was it?"

Marais took another slice of cake, leaving two for sharing.

"And then, Mr. Shirley?"

"Well, I watched Eve's first number and decided to stay on for the second."

"Would the nurse still come?"

"All that was forgotten by then, to tell the truth. I'd been knocking back a bit of plonk and that second act—not for your notebook, I think! You do get this down wonderfully fast."

"That's because I worked in the courts before joining the force."

"Really? That must be unusual. But where were we? Ah, yes. Her act ended and I was dying for a pee and shot down to the gents'. When I came out, it seemed everyone had gone, except Monty, having problems with that idiot who eats Mau Mau for breakfast. I certainly didn't want to become involved in that, so I slunk out down the other side and got safely to the door. What a relief. That man—"

"What about the band?"

"They'd gone, too. Always shoot out of the place—you should see them."

"And the time?"

"Couldn't tell you exactly. Five past? Something like that."

Marais broke off from his shorthand to print that in block letters.

"Not finished yet, Sergeant? Has someone near and dear been dragging my name in the mud?"

Marais glanced toward the door and grinned.

"Nearly. It's just Stevenson left us a message with his suicide note saying, 'Why not ask Shirley' on it."

"How peculiar!"

"It doesn't mean anything to you?"

"No. Does it to you?"

"Honest, it's got me floored. Same goes for the lieutenant,

and the colonel. Not something to do with Eve perhaps—Miss Bergstroom?"

Shirley poured Marais another cup while he thought it over, and then one for himself.

"Ah! I think I've got it. I'm in that note perhaps because of something Monty confided to me that same night, all very hushhush. Saw I was alone and came over for a few words. We got started on a bottle together and, after bitching generally about women, he said he wouldn't include Miss Bergstroom in this because he felt he'd formed—and I quote—a 'beautiful little relationship' with her. Ever met his wife? God, quite unbelievable. Poor old Mont—quite a little poppet in his own way."

Marais flicked back the pages to where he had recorded his interviews with Mrs. Shirley and the girl.

"Now, just quickly, the section after you left the club, so we've got it all cut and dried," he said.

Not one detail of what followed differed from what Marais had already been told. Shirley had been at home, after a twenty-minute drive from town, at 12:30 A.M., and asleep by about 1 A.M. It was all as simple as that.

11

Wessels stood awkwardly in his new beige safari jacket and shorts, white at the knees, pink about the neck where the clippers had been, looking like something out of a Lucky Strike packet.

"Come on, son," said Kloppers, wanting to get his van loaded and back to town before sunset—he'd been complaining about the state of its headlights for ten minutes.

"Ja, I'm pretty sure it's him," Wessels murmured.

The head of the body at his feet had ears that stuck out slightly and, when held up properly by Nxumalo, something of a flatness to the back of its skull.

Kramer touched the jacket with his toe.

"And that looks the same color, only I thought it was a bit darker."

"Right. Now again at the other one."

Wessels went over to the metal tray already in its catches on the floor of the van and fiddled with his new fringe.

"The shirt, but the head—well, it could be anyone."

"Thanks," said Kramer, and he went back to rejoin Zondi, who was leaning against the Chev. "He's pretty sure about the driver, less about the other. They'd not been boozing."

Zondi looked up at the high bank down which the old De Soto had plunged from one stretch of hairpin road to another, crashing on its nose and then rolling.

"Not so difficult," he said.

"Ja, we all know you're something of an expert in these matters, only you were lucky not to break your bloody neck."

"Dr. Strydom has come?"

"Never! He'll see them later in the morgue, but that's what it looks like. They must have been going full tonk, thinking there was no other traffic around here."

140

Zondi sighed contentedly. He'd been promised the dead sheep, and it was already in the trunk.

Kramer picked up the passbooks and driver's license that lay on the hood and looked at the names again: Mpeta and Dubulamanzi. These two were going to have had all the answers and correct papers for a spot check.

"This 'Dubulamanzi' crops up all over the place, hey? You even see it on sailing boats up at the dam."

"It means Parter of the Waters, boss. Also the name of the chief who gave the English their big hiding at Isandhlwana and Rorke's Drift."

"Uh, huh. Makes a come-down to a small-time crook. Did you ever think it was him?"

"Good driver. I remember from when he had a pirate taxi; six times the uniformed chased him. Mpeta is just a mad dog; many will be very happy when they hear he is dead."

"If he'd used guns before, we should have had him on file."

"No proof. You remember at the beer hall? When that old man was shot in a fight and everyone ran away? That time the informers said it was him, but Sithole and me can't get one person to talk."

"Why do you think they didn't pick up anything about these two? I mean, they're right in Peacevale."

"Maybe they are cleverer than we think. They don't spend their money; they just wait a bit."

"The switch to the De Soto wasn't bad; last thing I'd try and make a bloody getaway in. It's this mixture of clever and stupid I just don't get about these two, but I suppose that's exactly what we always rely on."

"He is ready now, boss," Zondi said, pointing to Tomlinson of Fingerprints, who had just completed his scene-of-accident pictures.

They walked across to the wreckage as Kloppers drove off, taking Wessels back with him. The kid's cockiness got a lot on Kramer's nerves.

"Sorry to mess around, sir, but the light's getting bad," Tomlinson said. "You can chuck it around now if you want to."

Kramer did not want to. A strange reluctance to learn more, to confirm what was already much more than a mere suspicion, held him back. For once the truth was totally without any appeal, and he wondered why.

"You look," he said to Zondi.

"Ja, I wouldn't like to put my hands in there," agreed Tomlinson, offering Kramer a cigarette. "Blood doesn't worry me the same way."

Then he supplied a light and they stood in silence for a while, looking out over the hill and listening to the night insects finding the right key.

"You've still got the sketch plan to do?" asked Kramer.

"A real waste of time that will be. Luckily the sergeant from the station down there has already done the measurements. You know, we had a member of the public in the other day to look at some shots, and he was surprised that even a coon killed in a back yard gets the full treatment. Nice bloke, came from Germany, but only been here six months. We showed him the docket on that butcher and he was amazed—all the plans, pics, and so forth. Said he could help us out with our reticulation problem maybe. Leicas come from there, don't they?"

Zondi had just lifted something out of the car and laid it on the grass.

"Hey? Ja, so I believe."

"Is there something the matter, sir? Your guts or—y'know?"

"Tired," said Kramer.

Zondi had just laid something else on the grass; it looked like a small toffee tin. He seemed as happy as a kid playing mud pies.

"You can say that again," sighed Tomlinson. "I'm for home as soon as this lot is finished."

Then Kramer had to know.

He walked down the slope, jumped a small aloe, and stopped beside Zondi's crouching figure. On the grass lay a long-barreled .22 pistol, its cracked butt wrapped with adhesive tape, and a wad of notes that was being carefully counted.

"How much?" he asked, as Zondi replaced them in the tin.

"Eighty-six rand, some change, and a coin I do not know."

He handed it up for inspection.

"Centavos? That's Portuguese."

"*Hau!*"

142

"Probably kept in the till for good luck or something. I'll ask sometime. Where was all this stuff?"

"Up underneath the front seat on the passenger's side. It was not easy to find, but it came loose in the crash so when I pressed hard on top I hear it knocking. There is also this."

And Zondi produced a small box of .22 rounds, high velocity, which he placed beside the pistol.

"I wonder where they thought they were going with this lot?" Kramer murmured, realizing that his reluctance to face the truth lay in its having solved a problem without supplying any real answers.

His mood must have been catching. Zondi dropped the tin and rose wearily, dusting grass and chips of shattered windshield from his trousers. And together they stood there, making a last check over a scene so mundane and familiar, from their separate years in uniform, that its recurrence then as something important to them seemed like a dirty trick. The glass, the twisted chrome trimmings, the hubcaps and discarded shoes, rags and an air filter, the smell of oil and petrol and battery acid, the subtle reek of accidental death . . .

Suddenly Kramer grabbed Zondi's arm and pointed.

Gardiner saw what the lieutenant meant the moment he swung open the double doors of the main refrigerator. The pair of feet, from which a label bearing the name Mpeta stuck out at a jaunty angle, were uncommonly small.

"It's after seven," Klopers nagged at his elbow. "I forgot to tell Nxumalo to stay, so if you need any help I suppose I'll have to."

"No sweat," said Gardiner, feeling the sole of each foot to test its moistness, "I can do it from here."

Then laughed at his inadvertent pun.

"The wife is getting bloody sick of this, I tell you."

"Pass me that roller, please. Ta."

"What has yours got to say?"

"Plenty."

"Exactly how long will this take?"

"*Ach,* just a minute or two, Sarge, and then I've got to go back to the office and use the glass."

Gardiner spoiled the first pull, and reached for another form.

"Any progress on the little girlie on the right?"

"Coming along, I hear. Marais was in the canteen tonight and he told me that he's cleared the first list of obvious suspects, none of the club members or guests involved, all cast-iron alibis. Seen them all except one who wasn't available, but he's covered by others. So now I suppose they'll have to start delving back into her lurid past."

Kloppers touched the label marked "Stevenson" and actually took a lively interest for an instant.

"Things are never so simple," he said.

Kramer thought otherwise. Anger was gradually filling the vacuum left by Zondi's departure for Peacevale, carrying with him the curious knowledge that Mpeta had been on Lucky's back doorstep, and in his bare feet. A vacuum because nothing, no new ideas or conjecture, could exist in it before fresh information was introduced. Gardiner's phone call had quite numbed him as well.

So it was good to have some feeling back, and he let it grow greedily on the rows of neatly typed words before him. Marais was outstandingly efficient in some respects, but in others a total bloody fool.

"Christ almighty," Kramer said softly.

"Sir?" answered Marais, who had hung on patiently for his pat on the back.

"This part of Shirley's statement beginning: 'I'm in that note perhaps because of . . .'"

"Ja? Stevenson wanted to corroborate that his personal attitude to the deceased was . . ."

And there he paused, aware of something wrong.

"You don't state your question, but that reply looks to me as if Shirley was allowed to know we had nothing up our sleeve—and, in fact, the exact context of our inquiry. Were you conspiring to assist a suspect, by any chance?"

Marais reddened and said, "I wasn't trying to help him, sir!"

"Oh, no? It didn't give him a chance to make up any rubbish he liked? Knowing we couldn't verify the hearsay of a dead man?"

"I thought . . . that it would make him tell the truth, sir, honest. As if we already knew and were pretending so we could check—"

"Marais! You didn't think at all, did you?"

Kramer had time to light a Lucky before the painful admission was made: Marais had not thought.

"Did it really matter, though, sir?"

"You ask me that?"

"But it isn't as though I knew nothing. I'd already got the first statements and his alibi was right there, in my book. His mother says he made her very angry by waking her at twenty-five past twelve to say he'd had a lousy night and was therefore going to join his friends who were staying in the mountains, leaving early."

"The time is very exact."

"I've got it all there, sir. She says she was angry, so she took her watch from the bedside table to see what the time was. She sleeps with pills, she said, and doesn't like being wakened."

"Uh-huh."

"Then the Bantu female Martha said she was awakened in her *kia* by the young master knocking on her door. He wanted her to make him an early breakfast, so he asked for her clock to adjust it, set the alarm for six, and went inside again. As she was closing her *kia* door, she saw in the light from the yard that it was one minute or so after twelve-thirty. She got up at six, ran his bath at quarter past, gave him his food at seven, and saw him leave the property at seven-thirty."

"Haven't they got a cook boy?"

"She is the cook, sir; used to be the nanny. Why?"

"Surely she would be up at six anyway."

"On Sunday in a lot of those houses, the people don't get up until after the Jo'burg papers come, so the servants have it easy, too. The Dragon, for example—"

"Hey?"

"Mrs. Shirley, I mean—she was fast asleep until just before lunchtime. She doesn't eat breakfast on Sunday but 'keeps herself,' so she puts it, for dinners with friends or at the club."

"Where's the husband all this time?"

"The ex-judge is away at Umfolozi Game Reserve."

"Ex-judge, hey?"

"Late of the Appellate Division," Marais said glibly.

Kramer glared.

It was a toss-up between kicking the bastard hard in the

arse, or trying to get something into his thick skull. Less satisfyingly, better judgment had the coin land heads and not tails.

"Sergeant, pull over Zondi's stool and sit down. You and me are going to have a bit of a little talk. I want you to forget about the note for a moment. If Shirley is clean, it won't have mattered; if he isn't, then it can be an advantage to seem half-witted while the other guy thinks he's smart."

"Er—ta, sir."

"Good. Go on, sit. You seem impressed by this man."

"He is polite and friendly, even. Really listens when you talk."

"Have you met a coolie who don't try to grease you like that?"

"Hey?" said Marais, shocked.

"And this part where you say he went out to the cook girl's *kia* to get the clock and tell her about the morning—why didn't he shout for her? Is he a liberal?"

"Progressive party maybe—in his position he couldn't be anything banned."

"*Ach,* we're not talking political parties now! This isn't Security! I asked you a straightforward question. Yes or no?"

"He treats the girl—well, perhaps he is a bit liberal; not in the suspicious sense, though."

"Since when is liberalism not suspicious until proven otherwise?" Kramer asked, missing the ashtray. "Nine times out of ten you'll find it's a university poop who can't make it with his own, so he uses liberalism to bring himself into the company of females who are automatically flattered by his interest. Ja?"

Marais nodded, and then said with a hopeful smile, "It can't be like that with the cook girl, Lieutenant. She's built like a bloody postbox and old enough to—"

"Look! We haven't time for jokes! This is a murder investigation, man! We are looking for motivation and all that crap. Are you with me now?"

"Sorry, sir."

"And in all this socializing you've been doing, have you met up with any young ladies that know this Shirley?"

"Only the one. The others had already checked out. She said Shirley wasn't her cup of tea; too like a cat, actually—only does what you want if it pleases him. She said she'd

146

not even glanced his way more than once."

"Interesting this was a blind date he was waiting for."

"I was surprised; he talks like a ladies' man but it seems he puts them off."

"And didn't this Eve—Sonja Bergstroom—have a dark skin?"

"It was—ja, a proper tan. But her identity—"

"(Or is this too subtle for you?) We're talking about how she seemed in his mind."

Kramer watched the dawn of insight spread pinkly up from Marais's collar. The man was not such a bloody fool after all. Nor was that too bad on his part, given the facts.

According to custom, the body of the butcher had been placed across one corner of the living room, screened off by a sheet. A saucer lay on the floor before it, already fairly well off for cash offerings toward the family's welfare and the funeral.

Zondi, who had called in not entirely out of respect, nonetheless placed a rand note with the rest and backed away.

"That is not all of it," the widow said bitterly, her face hidden by a black cloth.

The white priest from England, who had shown Zondi his permit to enter Peacevale, as if he cared, led her into another room, where the beds had been pushed aside to give the mourners standing space. There were many men there, mostly small traders with waistcoats and black armbands, each holding his hat to his chest and speaking in very low tones.

They avoided Zondi's direct look, and he felt angry—but whether at them or with himself he couldn't be sure.

"Stay well, my brothers," he said.

"Go well," they answered in a mumble.

This was no place for questions.

Outside, by the light of the streetlamp on the corner, children were playing in the yard. He paused to watch them.

"Ee-search, ee-search!" they shouted out, and ran off shrieking into the shadows, banging into tin fences and knocking over buckets and setting the fowls asquawk. Their panic had the full-bloodedness of make-believe. For some years yet he'd just be a bogeyman, and with such were the best night games played.

Zondi growled and flapped his arms, sending them shrilling delightedly across five properties or more.

Then he trudged up the smooth, worn bank to the gate where his car was parked, wondering where next to turn in his search for the identity of the third man, the one who had come from the car, the real killer. Because that was what his arithmetic made of the sole-print puzzle—and besides, Mpeta had not been a very convincing choice as a gunman.

He saw two youths peering in through his driver's window, and was about to send them packing with a boost of genuine fright when he recognized the taller of the two as Jerry, eldest son of Beebop Williams. He had been looking for him.

"You like cars?" Zondi asked.

"Very much, Sergeant!"

"Who is this one, Jerry?"

"His father is the dead man inside—his name is Thomas."

"You worked in your father's shop, too?"

"I am standard six," Thomas replied proudly.

"But these are school holidays, are they not? Or are you so educated that shopwork is not for you?"

"He works for another man, by the deposit-down bazaar, doing all his sums for him."

"Once I did work for my father," Thomas added, drawing numbers in the dust on the fender. "But he said I was not a white child who goes to school for free, and that I must earn the money for the fees and the books; he can use a stupid boy instead to ride the bicycle. I must go now. My greetings to your family, Jerry, and my thanks that you will walk with me tomorrow."

He meant at the funeral, and this caught his throat in a way that made him duck and run.

"If you are not ashamed of being thought arrested," Zondi said to Jerry, unlocking his door, "then you can ride with me—I will pass your house."

With a chortle of pleasure, Jerry slid across the seat, bounced on it to test its springs, and began fingering every knob and lever. He pulled at a steel ring on the underside of the dashboard and was bewildered to find it welded fast.

"For cuffs," explained Zondi, taking off slowly in case younger enthusiasts were underneath examining the substructure.

148

And the uneven road, rutted by bus tracks during the recent rains, kept their speed down for the rest of the hill. The right moment was chosen carefully.

"Tell me, Jerry, but where were you when Yankee Boy was with your father?" he said, dodging three daredevils naked up to their belly buttons, and giving no hint of having heard of the beating. "I suppose it was with the girls across at the dress house. Or was it with the others who wash clothes in the stream?"

"*Hau!*" the youth gasped.

"Which?"

"The dress house."

"Would you like me to drive round the top side?"

"Please—that would be special!"

"And on your way back, can you remember what you saw?"

Jerry flopped an arm over to hang down behind the seat, crossed his bare legs, put a foot against the dashboard, and began to whistle between his teeth.

"He cannot remember," Zondi chided gently, not wanting to drive a dream away. "He who looks so smart and so clever, as if I was his chauffeur man and he Dr. Pentecost."

His passenger chortled again. "When the one Sithole asks me, he says I have a very clear sight of things but I talk too much."

"You try to escape me. The truth is your memory is very, very bad."

"Huh!"

"What color was the car?"

"Red, Sergeant. I remember when it stopped there because I thought there would be trouble if they entered my father's shop and he wanted me to find a seventy-eight—the car was not so smart, you see? Then the stupid boy from next door, who works for Thomas, he comes up on his bike and says my father was shouting at the back for me."

"And so?"

Zondi handed over one of two cigarettes he had just lit in his mouth, and Jerry lay back, taking quick sucks at it, and closing his eyes.

"I cross the road and see one man in the car and I go sideways so my father can't see me. There are two old women talking over there, and there is an old man with a

149

donkey cart the other side. The bus has just been to take away people by the stop, and there is a woman with a baby on her back, packing her suitcase again because it broke open when dropped from the top of the bus."

"Hmmm. Your memory is not so wonderful, after all."

"Let me finish," Jerry said indignantly, settling back again. "I am in the road. Then I go down the path very carefully, because maybe my father is again looking for me. So I am crouching low, just like a dog, through the weeds, round by the broken car. I take a peep. *Hau!* I see white shining and I know it is my father's shirt. But next time I look, I see it is only one of those men who come from the hospital when the doctors are finished with them and throw them out. He is looking for food in the rubbish box, and I hide in case my father comes out to chase him away. Then, when he has gone to look in another place, I again go like a dog and I get right to the door, and I put my hand on the knob, turning it so quiet nobody can hear, and then in I go. Yankee Boy Msomi is there and I greet him and we talk together a little. He is a big friend of mine."

Zondi accelerated onto the divided highway and brought the needle up to the legal limit, then beyond, winding down his window to make the most of the rush of air. The arm swung around from behind the seat, and Jerry gripped the handle on the dashboard, pressed his forehead right against the windshield, and started clicking his tongue, urging them on even faster.

He was half a kilometer late in noticing they had passed his turnoff.

"Do we go somewhere else first?" he shouted hopefully.

"If you are not afraid."

"Me? I am a man!"

Someone else drove him home again from the mortuary, very subdued, if materially richer for his experience.

Marais was still trying to justify his technique when Kramer left the building in response to Zondi's honk from the street.

"Look, man—first thing tomorrow we'll make another start," Kramer said. "I'm getting a lift from that bloke over there."

"All the best," replied Marais, stopping to put on his bicycle clips.

Kramer knew exactly who Zondi meant.

"Uh-huh. You don't get so many, but I've seen them," he said as they started for home; both needed sleep badly. "The boys from the reserves and to-hell-and-gone who get discharged but haven't the moola to get home again. Live off charity and bugger around in dirt bins until uniformed picks them up on vagrancy and pass charges."

"The same. Many with no shoes when they come, many without shoes when they go—they sell them to buy sweets and cold drinks in the hospital, and there are the black-bitch nurses who make men pay for their lavatory basins."

"Zondi, I like this."

"Where are these persons most commonly seen, boss? At the back of the stores where the rubbish is. How close does anyone look at them? Not close. It can make you feel ashamed inside, but you have not the money for the whole world. What if I tell you a young man tonight identified Mpeta as such a scavenger outside the butcher shop?"

"Man, man, man!"

"There is more; you wait. To double-check, I went first to the station commandant, and he says they have had no prisoner answering the same description in regard to height and so on. In truth, I think they are giving these men an easy time these days. To double-double-check, I saw three people at the scenes of other incidents, who now remember such a man, wearing big bandages on his arms, who they have not seen again. One said he didn't notice dogs, so why ask such a strange question?"

Zondi stifled a yawn and squeezed his eyes shut once to clear them. The tar ahead widened, forked, narrowed, swept in through the gates of the township and ended abruptly behind the superintendent's office in a judder of potholed dirt. Then the trees gave out, too; there were just the endless rows of two-roomed Monopoly houses to show by their juxtaposition where the tracks lay. Kramer found he still counted each passing row carefully.

A door opened and closed quickly across the way as they stopped outside 2137.

"There are sixteen in that place," Zondi said, smiling. "They think old Mr. Tchor-tchor is paying them a visit."

Kramer winced at the evocative name for the bustling

151

superintendent, and muttered, "But what are your thoughts?"

"Exactly that, boss—a lookout. These stores are not white stores with a padlock on the back, but places where the children run in and out, boys forget to close doors, men go and stand in them for the sun. So there is this danger, if you do a raid, that someone will come in the back entrance and see you. But if you put a lookout there, who can beg from those that may wish to enter, then it is safe. That man can just run away by himself."

"Huh! Half-baked, man."

"Maybe, boss, but the yeast is blood."

Candlelight came to warm the window of 2137, drawing Zondi's hand to the door handle. His stomach rumbled.

"Bloody cannibal," said Kramer.

And drove away confident that the whole thing could be reshaped in the morning—along with a few destinies, if need be. Fatigue has its own euphoria.

12

Thursday's child was a great improvement on the rest of the week. Piet was out shooting with his new air rifle before the sun was properly up.

"Just listen to that," the Widow Fourie said, as Kramer brought in their coffee and sat on the edge of the bed.

Another swinging bottle burst at the end of its string in the old barn.

"How was he last night?" asked Kramer, whom nothing could have wakened.

"Got much more sleep, but still a bad dream now and then during the early part. I wish you'd listen so I had your opinion."

Kramer pretended to leave the room and she threw a pillow at him.

"You tell me, then," he said, stretching out, already fully dressed, beside her.

A praying mantis on the windowsill crossed from one side to the other.

"Well, it's these books."

"Uh-huh."

"You see, the more I read them, the more I think Piet has got Oedipus."

"Hoo!"

"No; you wait. Doctors aren't always right!"

"Okay, okay. You've got all morning until eight o'clock."

The Widow Fourie tucked the pillow back behind her head and looked up at the high, old-fashioned ceiling with its plaster trimmings, just like a wedding cake, and tried to find the right words.

"It's like this: Piet was at *the* age when it happened—y'know?"

"Uh-huh."

"That's what the books call becoming fixated by a trauma event. Bereavement is all you need for it to happen. Now, it was natural at that age for Piet to be jealous of—y'know."

"His dad."

"Ja, and it was also natural he should want rid of Pop with death wishes and the like."

"Mmmm."

"You haven't heard all this before, because it's a new part I found in *The Rib Cage*. It says that the child realizes that if his father found out how he feels, then there would be big trouble. That the father would punish the son—which is easy to do because he's so much bigger. The kiddie mixes two things, you see, this pash for his mum and this fear his dad will cut off his—y'know."

"*Tondo?*"

"Hell, the words Mickey teaches you!"

"That's right, blame a poor kaffir," he said, nudging her.

"Tromp, seriously, man, listen to my reasoning. So, in the classic examples, the kiddie tries to be very nice to his dad, to sort of make up for wanting him dead. They say you can see this in a normal boy when he switches over to worshiping his dad at a later stage."

"So if he gets stuck at this point, he develops a phony attitude of liking his dad while really he—"

"Hey! We're talking about Piet here, so that's beside the point."

"Piet," affirmed Kramer.

"And you know what *I* think is the matter with him? He thinks he's a murderer!"

The coffee spilled hot down Kramer's shirt as he sat bolt upright.

"What bloody nonsense is this?"

"And that's why you have an effect on him the doctors are always talking about. They don't understand it, but I do. Piet knows who you catch—and what happens to them in Pretoria."

"You mean . . . ?" Kramer went over and stripped off the stained shirt, replacing it with another taken from his suitcase in the wardrobe. Then he turned on her.

"You listen," he said. "I read those books, I saw the ideas on psychopaths. I'll accept all this crap for a moment just to point out to you that they said the important years were

154

up to five. For those years, was there any messing around with Piet? Didn't you have him by your side the whole time? Didn't you hug him and teach him his empathy and everything? You told me yourself you only got a girl when you had to go out to work after he died. Before then, Piet had—"

The Widow Fourie was staring open-mouthed at him.

"Isn't that what you mean, then?" he said, coming over and taking her empty cup from her.

"I never said my Piet was a psychopath!"

"*Ach,* they go together! Oedipus and early—"

"Only in the case of the psychopath himself, you damn fool! *Please listen!*"

"Fine," said Kramer, banging the cup down on her dressing table. "Piet thinks he's a murderer. Who did he kill?"

"His—his own Pop."

"*Yirra!*"

"See it from his point of view! He's little and he's wishing his dad dead so he can have me to himself—and what happens? His dad dies! What else would a kid think? You know how their heads are full of magic? How they can have friends that are just imaginary? Take strange fears? What's so unlikely then that at night he thinks the curtains are moving because his pa's spook is coming back to . . ."

Kramer slowly buttoned his shirt, did the cuffs, and slid up the knot in his tie.

"You're right—it was ghosts which were scaring Piet the other night when I went through to his room," he admitted, adding with a wry smile, "That's why I got him the gun to shoot them with."

The colonel brooded over the feature page of the *Gazette,* which had the headline SNAKES AND ADDERS bannered across it, and a blurb that read: "Snakes kill 35,000 humans a year—one such victim died tragically in Trekkersburg this week. But fangs ain't always what they seem, writes K. Madison, our Special Science Correspondent."

Then came the usual whispers, sharp knock, and cheery greetings that began the press call every day at eight-thirty.

He announced that two Bantu males, involved in the brutal attack on the Munchausen Café, had been killed in an accident making their getaway, and that both the money and the firearm had been recovered. This was followed by the details of two housebreakings, involving property worth about two hundred rand in each case, and he rounded off with the total numbers killed in a faction fight the previous weekend in the Tugela Valley—forty-two on one side, thirty-eight on the other, with ninety huts in all burned.

"That the lot, Colonel Muller?" asked the efficient one, stuffing his notebook away and leaning toward the door.

"That's the lot," he declared, "but I would like the gentleman from the *Gazette* to stay behind a moment, please. I'm interested to know who this Madison bloke is."

"Me," said one of them.

"But you're Mr. Keith, not so?"

The other reporters glanced at each other and fled from the room, their laughter echoing loud in the corridor.

"Er—Keith Madison, sir. Maybe there was some misunderstanding when I introduced myself."

"I see. Science as well as crime."

"And the films and the farming."

"Very nice," said the colonel. "Now tell me, just what are you driving at in this article?"

"In what way?"

"How aren't things what they seem?"

"Er—it's a question of attitudes. For instance, as you can read there, I found out for a fact that it's only in the West here, where we can have all the meat we like, that snakes aren't eaten extensively. They're protein for millions of pople—Asia, South America, Africa, India especially."

"Really? And you don't think this is a bit tasteless?"

The reporter brayed and said, "Oh, bloody good, sir!'

"Pardon?"

"I—we, that is—aren't really driving at anything. Just latching on to what's topical. The whole town's got snake fever—the girl's death really started something. The ecologists are very worried that with all the killing of snakes going on, the balance of—"

"Let me be frank with you, Mr. Madison, I am not happy with the way this thing is slanted. Did you write the letters, too? From so-called experts disputing that death could have been caused in the manner described in Tuesday's issue?"

"Oh, no, they're quite genuine. Apparently *Python regius* hasn't the—"

"*Ach!*"

156

"All right, Colonel. You're being frank, so I'll be, too," said the reporter, with the defiant air of a man in his finest hour. "A lot of questions are being asked. First, Eve has a fatal accident. Next, Monty Stevenson dies by his own hand in a police cell. Then your men start making intensive inquiries—and yet you issue no statement whatsoever about either death. That's four things that don't make two and two!"

"And so?"

His bluff called, the reporter sidled away, aware that he had a right only to information concerning fires or road accidents.

But the colonel got through to Kramer on the internal line and said, "Tromp, whatever your theories concerning the Peacevale gang, that team has now been broken up and so the matter goes into abeyance until you've got this Bergstroom docket closed. I'm not listening to any arguments—you've got that straight? I want all your men on it now, today, and you're to supervise the investigation until an arrest has been made or I'm satisfied that we have done all we can."

He put down the receiver with a firm hand and dragged over his In tray. Kramer's strange indifference to the girl and obsessiveness about the gang quite bewildered him—although once, just for an instant, he had sensed something that was impossible to put his finger on.

"Sorry, boss, no spoons," said Zondi, coming in with a tray and giving Kramer, Marais, and Wessels their cups of tea before retiring to the corner with his tin mug, filled to the brim by five helpings of sugar.

Marais cleared his throat noisily.

"No, Zondi had better hear something of this," Kramer said, taking a sip, "because I think he can help us decide whether Shirley can be eliminated and that list closed. There's no point in taking any other line until then."

"Help?" queried Marais.

"Servants can tell you more about a family than their own doctor, lawyer, and abortionist rolled into one."

"Hmmm."

"Will you outline the position for Constable Wessels, please?"

Marais summed up Mrs. Shirley's statement.

"You have only the word of a mother, Sergeant, sir?" asked Zondi.

"Don't be stupid," said Marais. "That's what your boss means. The girl also says she was woken within five minutes of that time. Would she tell lies?"

Zondi shrugged.

"It's just I don't think Mickey will get far with this Martha, sir. One of the loyal types, if you ask me, with her bum right in the butter. Mrs. Shirley told me she'd been with the family since their one and only was five, after lots of different nannies before, who were all rubbish. And they'd made her the cook girl afterwards so she wouldn't leave them."

"Well, Zondi?" Kramer prompted, accepting Wessels's offer of a wet pencil to stir with.

"Maybe, if her life was very sweet, she would tell a lie—but it is hard to explain to your maid why she should do this. Also, a black person is more afraid of the police."

"That sounds to me," said Wessels, "like an argument in favor of doing as Sergeant Marais says and accepting this evidence."

"True, Constable, but Sergeant Marais and me have already had one experience this week that taught us a lesson about evidence supplied by womenfolk—am I right?"

"Hell, now I see why there's doubt in your mind!" Marais exclaimed.

Ironically, it was also Kramer's own moment of enlightenment. Up until then, distracted still by the gang killings, he had been playing this briefing by ear, allowing a line of attack to develop unquestioned. And yet now, even more ironically, negative doubts took over.

"Hold on," he said, and went out onto the courtyard balcony to weigh retreat against advance.

The wife of an ex-judge was a very different matter than that of a sleazy caterer. This did not mean, however, that she wouldn't lie to protect her son. A son who had been specifically mentioned in connection with the deceased's death. An only child who had no alibi other than that provided with suspicious precision by his mother—and by a servant who could be influenced. And a basic requirement

158

of routine investigation was that all grounds for suspicion should be eliminated.

Simple.

He waited. But no feeling came; it all stayed in his head, as insipid as checkers jumbled in their box when the board was set for chess.

"*Ach*, I just don't want to know," Kramer muttered to himself, and realized that was the truth of it.

Then he remembered the button.

"But, Lieutenant," protested Marais, half a minute later, "shouldn't we work on the relationships first? You want me to see about the shirt at this stage? When only she's at home?"

"Routine elimination," said Kramer, putting his feet up on the desk. "A nice hard little fact for you to play with."

"Ja, maybe."

"Do both. Zondi, you go and get the button from the safe while Sergeant Marais gets his car. You, Wessels, you're the undercover specialist; you go and uncover something."

"Like what, sir?"

"Background. Now, let's get this show on the road."

And when the office had emptied, he decided that the Peacevale problem was very like that trick done with three bottletops and a pebble, only you had to guess which the gun was under.

Martha opened the front door to the timorous tap Marais gave on the big brass knocker.

"Is your missus in?"

"She is lying down, master; I think she is asleep. Do you wish me to disturb her?"

"Hang on a— She's asleep, you say?"

Martha nodded.

"Do you think she'd mind if I just came in and saw something? Just quickly?"

The girl was looking very dubious about this when there was a creak and a thud from the room above the hall. Marais slipped his hand into his pocket to gain reassurance from the button in its plastic packet, much as he might from a rabbit's foot.

It wasn't there.

"The missus is coming," said Martha.

"Look, is my boy round the back where I told him?"

"There is a man there."

"Then go quickly and ask him to give the button to you—go on. And bring it here, *che-che.*"

"Oh, you've come to pry again, I see," Mrs. Shirley said from the stairs. "And where do you think you're going, Martha? You haven't finished the dusting, have you?"

The tone she used on the servant instantly dispelled any idea of a liberalist bond between them.

"Look, Mrs. Shirley—"

"Martha?"

"He has a man at the back he told me to fetch a button from, madam."

"A man at the back?"

"He's only my boy," Marais said hastily, "and he was thirsty so I sent him round to the kitchen to ask for water."

Martha raised her brows slightly but said nothing to further embarrass him.

"Don't stand about, girl!"

As Martha took her feather duster upstairs, Mrs. Shirley, more witchlike than dragonish in her long black house gown, came soundlessly off the bottom step.

"That servant is not here to be at your beck and call!"

"I'm sorry. Is she the only—" began Marais, before freezing at the folly of his abject words.

"What impertinence! You're in this house five seconds and you're trying to interrogate me!"

"No, honest, lady, I wasn't getting at you or anything."

"When my husband, *Justice* Shirley, takes his annual holiday and there is no entertaining to do, the general domestic staff take theirs. Martha is perfectly capable of seeing to the needs of Peter and myself—but not of the entire South African Police Force. Do I make myself clear?"

"Yes, lady, I'm sorry, hey?"

"And this is a perfectly ridiculous time to call. My son would hardly be in at midday."

"That's okay with me. I've only come to look at something."

"Oh?"

"The lieutenant sent me. You can phone him if you like."

Mrs. Shirley deliberated this for a moment.

"Well? Look at what?"

"It's routine elimination—shirts—and we're going to do it to everyone eventually."

"Show me the search warrant."

She moved to stand across the foot of the stairs; he had seen this done in westerns. It made him feel suddenly taller and more certain of himself.

"Search warrants, Mrs. Shirley, are only signed by a magistrate if there is positive evidence, or if we are hindered in carrying out a normal process of elimination for reasons that appear suspicious."

Or something like that; but it worked. He could almost see her come down a peg or two.

"What sort of shirts? Surely not all of them?"

"No, the tuxedo kind."

"Dress shirts, I suppose you mean?"

"Those. So I'll just—"

"You, young man, are not setting a foot farther into this house. I am perfectly capable of bringing them to you."

And she swept soundlessly up the stairs.

Leaving Marais flushed and confused, with a sinking feeling that sank even deeper when he shoved both hands into his pockets and found his left one close on the button.

"Oh, *yirra*," he said, realizing then that Zondi must have dutifully slipped it into the jacket as it lay bunched on the car seat beside him—and that any hope of blaming the bastard for the boob he'd made had gone.

Which gave him the impetus he needed to race after Shirley's mother and make sure she didn't try anything.

Zondi and the dog regarded each other with a mixture of deep loathing and some respect.

They had been sitting like that, eye to eye, water dish to plastic cup, ever since Mrs. Shirley had come down to see they both stayed in the yard. She had handed Zondi the water without a word before disappearing again. It was a strange place.

Then Martha Mabile came back to join him.

"Pooma!" she said to the dog, and it slunk over to lie under a granadilla vine that screened the yard from the garage.

"So life goes," said Zondi, recognizing in her all the signs of a good churchwoman.

"Is the young master in big trouble?" she asked.

"You think they tell me?" Zondi asked, laughing sourly. "Huh! I am that sergeant's driver, that is all. Maybe he stole something."

"Don't you speak of the young master like that! What are you? A lazy donkey that carries other men on his back. I have been with the master since he was so high, like a small boy, and he is a kind man."

"What is his name?"

"Master Peter. But he has been the young master many years now."

Again Zondi smiled, amused by the convention that required nannies to cease calling a child by name once he had become a boy no longer to be ordered about.

Martha softened, and handed over half an orange.

"*Hau, hau, hau,* but he was a real *skabenga* when he was small, that one. I am very glad that now he has grown up. Then he takes his pellet gun or the catapult and shoot, shoot everywhere. He climbs trees so he falls down and hurts himself, he is always hungry, a lot of work and trouble. And he is cruel with other children that come here to play and I have to smack him hard!"

"The madam let you hit him?"

"Shhhhh! She would go mad if she heard I touch him! But you know how I did it? I hit him underneath the foot so she would see no marks."

Zondi applauded her cunning with a guffaw. "Did he never tell his mother you did this?"

"Of course, many times. But I would say, 'Me, madam? You want to give me my notice?' And she would say, 'That's another fib, Peter—get out of my sight.' Fib is her word for an untruth."

"And this child is now truly a good man?"

Martha giggled and spat out a pit.

"He is always with the young women," she said. "Now it is peaceful."

Then Marais shouted from the driveway, "Mickey! Come on, man, where the hell are you?"

"You should smack under his feet," Martha confided in a whisper.

The memo lay on the colonel's blotter, pinned down by the

point of his paper knife like a venomous flatfish.

"The brigadier has gone so far as to put it in writing, Kramer."

"Oh, ja?"

"I thought just a friendly phone call this morning would be enough for you to take a personal interest in the case."

"In what way wasn't it, Colonel?"

"In here the brigadier says he has just had a very unpleasant little conversation with a friend of the attorney general's."

"Uh-huh?"

"Mr. Justice Shirley, late of the Supreme Court, and the husband of a very upset lady, he says. The judge is driving down from Zululand now for an appointment with the brigadier at four-thirty. It seems one of your men has been to his house and made a real nuisance of himself."

"Can you tell me how?"

"Yes. He forced his way in and used threats on Mrs. Shirley to make her show him some shirts he wanted to compare with a button."

"*Hey?*"

"You know what I think is going to happen next, Kramer? We're going to have our little black friend Zondi arresting white suspects. It is coming to that."

The knife pressed right through the paper.

"I resent that, Colonel!"

"Not as much as I resent the fact that one of my senior officers saw fit to send an inexperienced subordinate in his place to conduct a most delicate inquiry. Resent? That's hardly the bloody word for it!"

Without asking leave, Kramer jerked away the memo.

"I see what the brigadier wants is a complete justification for our actions before the judge gets here," he said.

"That is almost irrelevant. You claim Shirley sticks out like a sore thumb, but from what else you tell me, you've still got a very long way to go—if you're traveling in the right direction in the first place. What inquiries, for instance, have been made at the deceased's boardinghouse regarding possible men friends in her life?"

"Wait—I'll go and see the lady myself."

"God in heaven!" bellowed the colonel. "Can't you even

read now? Nobody goes near her, Shirley, or the house until the brigadier—"

Then he, too, saw what lay between the lines.

And Kramer murmured, "Maybe Marais was the right man for the job after all, sir. He should be back soon."

13

The outburst in the office seemed to startle Wessels as much as it did Zondi.

"You sneaky black bastard!" stormed Marais, spinning around with his fist raised.

"Hold it right there, Sergeant," Kramer said quietly. "The girl mentioned nothing to him about the button. You can see from his face this is news to him."

"Then how—"

"From the horse's mouth—Mrs. Shirley. She's been bitching to the brigadier."

Zondi began a discreet withdrawal.

"You come back," Kramer ordered.

Marais took breath to protest, but had it knocked out of him by the next remark.

"Man, I think you did well there, even if she is screaming her panties blue."

"Sir?"

Kramer motioned for him to take his chair again, and then said, "Let's hear it all from the beginning."

"Her manner was very aggressive when I entered the premises," Marais began, after a long pause to collect himself. "She wanted to see my search warrant, but backed down when I said they were issued only in suspicious circumstances. . . . It was the girl to blame for telling her about the button actually."

"Uh-huh?"

"First Zondi put it in my wrong pocket and then—"

"*Ach,* no. What did Ma Shirley do next?"

Marais dithered and said, "You want it step by step? But I told you even with the button error I'm convinced—"

"Every detail," snapped Kramer.

"Okay. So she went up the stairs to call the girl and get

the shirts for me. She was still under suspicion at that stage, so I deliberately allowed her to think she could be giving me the slip. But I then followed right on her tail and found her in the suspect's bedroom in a state of agitation, saying she did not know where the dress shirts were kept."

"What interval did you follow at?"

"Only seconds, sir. Then she called the girl, Martha, to show her where to find them. I examined the shirts and found they were all in order, with no new buttons or signs of every button being changed. There were five shirts in all, and the girl verified this was the correct number. I felt therefore satisfied that the button did not belong to any of the suspect's shirts."

"What was her manner?"

"Aggressive, sir."

"Not nervous in any way?"

"I didn't see any reason to think so. It's just I think she has some kind of grudge against me—I don't know why."

"And you are positively certain she did not have time to conceal a shirt and to tip off the girl there were then only five?"

"The girl was working at the other end of the wing. It would have been impossible to reach her in the time I allowed her."

"But the girl, seeing there were five shirts, could simply agree this was the correct number—not wishing to cross swords with her employer or, as you say, have her bum removed from the butter?"

"There's no love lost between those two, sir; I can tell you that for a fact."

"Zondi?"

"She shows no respect, Lieutenant."

Marais lifted an upturned thumb at him and winked.

"Where were these shirts, Sergeant?"

"On a shelf in the wardrobe."

"Not difficult to see?"

"You know that sort of woman, sir. She wouldn't know where to find herself without—"

"So this could all be camouflage," Kramer said. "The shirt had already been taken care of, and this act with the servant was just to make you think she wouldn't know where to start, et cetera. Her attitude to the girl could be an act, too,

166

aimed at making us think it impossible she could have conspired with her over the times."

"Then I'd still have expected *some* reaction when the button first came up, but she seemed hardly to hear what the girl said."

"Like a twitch, you mean?"

Marais nodded his thick head.

"I think you see too many films," said Kramer, getting up to pace the floor. "Let's stick to basics that are with us in real life. We have a killer, and protecting a killer is a woman's job—wife, mother, girlfriend. Men do it, but only for money. Ma Shirley was the first member of the household interviewed."

"Ja."

"When that interview was over, did she have any opportunity of instructing the girl as to what she should say to you?"

"Um, I suppose she did. She went to fetch her from the kitchen."

"When she could have rung?"

"I didn't see a—"

"And was Shirley out of your hearing, and possibly in her company, before he made his statement to you?"

"He went to get some fresh tea."

"Sir, can I say something?" Wessels asked. "All this suggests the alibi was concocted on the spur of the moment. Why wouldn't Shirley and her have got it fixed up from the start?"

Kramer swung around and said with a smile, "Would you tell your ma you'd done a thing like that?"

"Christ, never!"

"But she's your ma, remember—wouldn't she guess you were in some kind of trouble?"

"A mother always knows," said Zondi.

And every man in the room showed he agreed with that.

Then Marais scratched his head to show his uncertainty implied no criticism and said, "Except she calls her son all those names and makes out she doesn't give a bugger for him."

"That's something Martha said," Zondi piped up. "How the madam was so quick to call the young master a liar and

167

send him away from her—that was when he was a small boy and did mischief."

"What mother doesn't do that at some time?"

"She seemed a hard woman, Lieutenant."

"They're all hard, up there. But can't you see? If she plays this up with us, doesn't that help her case even more?"

"True," said Wessels.

Kramer sat down again, drumming his fingers on the desktop, making everyone else stir restlessly.

"What else did you other two pick up?" he asked, pointing at Zondi to finish his turn first.

"Nothing special. She just talks of when the man was young and would do foolish things with his catapult."

Wessels laughed and said, "I bet she didn't tell you he once lobbed some bloody rocks at her in her *kia* when she was in bed with a bloke! That's all I got—from an old Bantu constable at the local cop shop. Does that count as a background of violence, sir?"

"There were actual injuries?" Kramer asked, smiling but interested.

"Oh, ja, and a hell of a shindig, but when uniformed got there the guy had buggered off with his war wounds. The usual old thing: he was on the premises illicitly without a permit. They say—What's up, sir?"

"Marais, you remember that car park where Stevenson had his own slot? Wouldn't a swanky-puss like Shirley—"

"Hell, that's a hell of an idea, sir! They've got a boy guarding it down at the entrance and sports cars are always something people notice! The time he left there?"

"You've got it. Find me that boy."

Kramer would have sent Zondi around with Marais, but the sensitive little sod had disappeared before anyone noticed—which wasn't at all strange in the circumstances.

Marais tried again. The wog was really giving him trouble. And people using the car park were watching.

"Were you, or were you not, on duty on Saturday night?"

"Aikona."

"But your boss says you were!"

"The manager says that? But he knows the shift is changing Sunday."

168

"Then who was on duty at half-past twelve—you understand that?"

Marais pointed out the exact position of the hands on his navigator's wrist watch, which the attendant much admired and offered three rand for.

"You answer me!"

"At that time, sir, it was me here on duty."

"Jesus H. Christ!"

"Amen, hallelujah," murmured the attendant, rolling his eyes.

Marais grabbed him by the lapels. "Look!"

"That is Sunday—not Saturday, sir."

"So you're a clever dick, hey? Think you're smart? Then I'll tell you something—you're under bloody arrest."

"Hau!"

The lieutenant's pet monkey could deal with him.

Kramer was caught right in the act.

"I heard from Wessels you'd got an idea to crack the alibi," the colonel said, sitting down on the corner of the desk. "But that didn't sound like this inquiry to me."

"Marais has been gone about half an hour, sir. If you like to wait a minute, maybe you'll hear the result." Kramer moved his hand casually from the telephone receiver he had just replaced in its cradle.

"And who were you talking to?" the colonel persisted.

"That? Just a nun I know."

"You let her ring you at work?"

Kramer's grin pleased the colonel and they both eased the tension.

"One of Funchal's daughters. I wanted to check on that centavos coin we found in the car yesterday, and asked for Da Gama. But he's taken over the business affairs and was away in Durban, so she told me instead, after asking her granny, that her father kept one in the till because it'd been blessed by an archbishop or something."

"Which clinches that," said the colonel.

"Uh-huh."

"But how about the button? I've heard nothing from you, and Wessels seems to think that the mother may not be running circles round us."

"It smells, sir. Really it does. And I'm not at all happy

169

about the time she really had in that bedroom before Marais joined her. That business about pretending he could be given the slip sounds a little too—"

"Talk of the devil," said the colonel, as Marais came in, red and bad-tempered.

"I've got the car-park boy downstairs, sir, and I need Mickey to question him—his English is bloody terrible."

"Ja, where is he?" asked the colonel.

Wessels wandered in and said, "Who?"

"Zondi."

"I don't know, sir.

"And you, Lieutenant?" growled the colonel. "Or is he doing a ballistics test up the road?"

At that moment, Zondi skidded in through the door.

"Where have you been?"

"Colonel, sir?"

"Explain your absence from this office."

"I've been to the Shirley residence, sir."

"*What?* To do what?"

"Make an arrest."

The colonel jumped to his feet. "No! *Who,* you madman?"

"Oh, just the mother of the young master."

Stunned, Kramer stared at him like everyone else, but seemed to see in his expression a smugness directed only at himself, as if a diffrence of opinion had now been settled most satisfactorily in the crazy bastard's own favor.

Martha Mabile sat, her hands together and limp in her lap, on the stool in the interrogation room, quite removed from her surroundings.

So the men looking down on her simply talked as though Martha were not there at all.

"I helped you?" Kramer asked.

"*Hau,* it was what you were saying about a mother's love, Lieutenant."

"*Ach,* no!" objected Marais.

"You mean about sharing the risks of deception?"

"Spot on, and there was wisdom also in the statements made by Sergeant Marais, for he has a sharp eye and he told us that he could see no liking between the missus and the

170

girl. Why should the girl stay at the house? She is clever and can get a good job somewhere else."

"Lots of nannies become cook girls," Marais broke in, to be silenced by the colonel's frown.

"So I think to myself: What has this woman told me? That the child was hungry, so she fed it; that it was hurt, so she cared for it; then a most loving thing—when it was bad, she gave it chastisement."

"That's what a nanny's for, stupid!"

"Marais . . ."

"Sorry, Colonel."

"And when," said Zondi, with the cautious tone of respect, "the child tells the missus that his nanny has beaten him, it is the nanny's word which is the truth, as is always the word of a mother, right or wrong."

Wessels asked, "What about all the other nannies?"

"They did not like him, because they could see no good—but Martha has eyes that go deep."

"So she pretended the kid was hers?"

"I have known many cases, Colonel. Even among the women who have little ones that must stay on the homeland."

"Hey, you know what this reminds me of?" Wessels said suddenly. "You remember when you played Rugby at a posh school? The cheering? The old wog girls who used to stand over behind the fence and say, 'Shiya sterek, Number Seven-a-teen, che-che!' "

"Say?" hooted Marais. "The way I remember, they were all bloody shouting! And you remember how the other side would walk off without looking, thinking we would say they were kaffir-love—hell, sorry, Colonel."

Kramer moved around to confront Martha, whose face was still as impassive as when she had been led into the room.

"Zondi, you're saying that Shirley told this woman his troubles—just like his mum?"

Martha laughed softly.

"No, you do not understand, sir. This is the cook girl who looks after him, putting food in his stomach. Would he not be very ashamed?"

"That's my point, man! How did she know to take the measures you accuse her of?"

"And she can't read or write," Marais added, "because

Shirley himself told me—what does she know of police procedures?"

"No, this I want to hear from her," Kramer decided.

Martha said something into Zondi's ear. He patted her on the shoulder and turned to the colonel.

"Her English is bad; she asks that I interpret."

"Fine, let's hear it!"

"Only in Afrikaans," Marais reminded him, taking out his notebook, "and in the first person."

"I still do not know why there is all this trouble with the young master," Martha began. "But when I see policemen come to the house and they are CID, then I am very afraid for him. I have this fear because of certain things I have noticed at the weekend that has just passed. The first thing is when Master Peter comes to my door in the middle of the night. He will usually call for me by the back door. I am so afraid that he will see my husband Aaron is sleeping with me, for he has no permit to be on the premises. So I go quickly to the door and when he asks for my clock I give it to him quickly also so he will not step inside. I think it is strange he does not tell me to change the hands, as this is a thing I have learned to do. Then I close the door and see that the time is just after half-past twelve, and I say to Aaron that the young master is home early for the weekend. Aaron says the clock is no good because his pocket watch says it is nearly one o'clock. We laugh then because I say to him, 'That old thing is no good,' and he argues, saying it has many jewels in it."

The colonel said just, "God!"

And the two voices went on. "In the morning I make the young master his breakfast and put it in the dining room, and while he is in the bath I go to tidy his room. Ever since he was a small boy, his room has been untidy and clothes just thrown on the floor. I take the dirty washing and I see his shirt has a button that I must find and put on. But although I look and look by the place where he undresses, there is no button fallen there so I think he has been with girls again. He boasts to me of such things to show me he is a man now. I brush his jacket, which has got a white mark on it, then I also notice . . ."

"What's up, Zondi?"

172

"*Hau*, she says this part is not for the ears of the white masters. Better she leaves it, for she is too shy and ashamed."

"Tell her we will not be angry."

Zondi, looking uncomfortable himself, persuaded her to continue.

"I have the young master's shirt and his undershirt and his socks and then I realize I do not have his underpants. So again I look on the floor and all around. Then I did a thing without thinking, for I had done it so many times long before."

"Keep going," said the colonel.

"When he was becoming a man, he would like to hide his pajamas under the mattress, like so, when in the morning he took them off. It was my instruction that pajamas must be placed under the pillow when the bed was made, so I searched hard until I discovered this was his habit. I think he did this because when in the night his dreams spilled seed and—"

"Okay, skip the history, Zondi."

"I found the underpants under the mattress and there was a little seed on them. But for a long time the young master had not been ashamed of such things, and I wonder what it is making him to do this. Then I think of what Aaron said about the clock, although it seemed I had woken the missus at the right time. Then the CID come and I am asked what time, what time, and I see that the clock was important in some way. I can choose to say only what the young master tells me, or what Aaron has said. But this is not trouble for Aaron, so I just say—"

"And the button?" asked Marais, dropping his pen.

"She was the one with all the time to shoot upstairs," Kramer said. "She had a quick look for the shirt, tricked Ma Shirley over the right number, and all without really knowing what the sod was going on."

Zondi spoke in Zulu to Martha and then confirmed this had been the sequence of events—although she had nearly been seen by her employer.

Marais got an attack of the old trouble and hastened off to the bog.

Martha said something else.

"She asks if she can now know what girl has made a complaint against her master," Zondi explained. "She is not stupid, this one."

"What we need now," said Kramer, rising to the surface, "is that husband of hers to testify about the time. Where does he live? Bloody Durban, I suppose?"

"*Hau*, no, Lieutenant. He is the first one I catch."

"Hey? How come?"

"The story Boss Wessels told about a man in her *kia* sounded strange in my ears, because I can see she is a church-woman and would not give away her favors."

"Where was he, then? You had only—"

"Right next door at number thirty-two. I said to him there would be no trouble about the permit offense this time if he was willing to be of assistance."

"Quite right," said the colonel, and then noticed it was half-past four.

Marais had been sent on his own to bring Shirley in for questioning, so Wessels shot over to the canteen to buy himself a quick Coke.

He was drinking it in the doorway, glorying in what he knew and yet had to keep to himself for the moment, when Warrant Officer Gardiner waved him over; then, realizing Wessels was armed and couldn't enter, actually made his way across to him.

"How's the case going?" Gardiner asked.

"Not bad at all, sir."

"Then you've found the third guy?"

"Oh, that one, you mean. We haven't had time for that business today. When I left CID to come over, the lieutenant had just started getting brainwaves that the shooting was done by the one at the back door."

Gardiner's eyebrows did their thing.

"Ja, and then there was the problem of where did the passenger go, and Mickey said why not under the dashboard?"

"I must be pissed," said Gardiner.

"No, even for a coon, that's logical. They used old cars, which still had the high doors, and there are no pavements in Peacevale to give passers-by the extra elevation, no double stories either. And as Kramer says, you count the number of persons in a vehicle by counting the heads, and if one suddenly goes you think you must have missed looking that way for a moment."

"Let's talk in the passage," said Gardiner, pushing Wessels out with a friendly poke in the belly. "Now try and explain this better where I can hear you."

"It's dead simple, the way he's got it now. The one round the back in the bandages—maybe they are even hiding the gun—arrives at the scene independently and on foot. The other two roll up in front of the shops, and the passenger gets his head down. It's the driver that keeps the lookout for when the pedestrian traffic drops, then he gives a honk like I heard him do, but the kaffirs are so used to their own kind doing noisy things like that they forget. And the shots have them—"

"And the one with the gun?"

"By that time, when the horn goes, he has found a shop that isn't being guarded at the rear. He goes in, looks round to see there are no customers, shoots the storekeeper, grabs the money, and he's out the back way while everyone is coming up off the grit watching the car tear away. Now even if that car hits a roadblock, the two in it have no money, no gun—nothing to worry them. And they meet up again later."

Gardiner shook his head.

"It's not all just imagination, sir. It seems that the lieutenant warned this Lucky bloke, for instance, and now he points out that Lucky was shot, not near his till, but up near the shopwindow, as if he'd seen the car and was watching it. Plus Doc Strydom said he'd been shot on the turn—the turn *towards,* not away, you see? And wouldn't Lucky have backed towards his till if the man came in the front? Just think how many times that car may have stopped at different places and the back doors were shut. Or they could have got the record shop instead of the butcher—maybe that was their intention. Pot luck, Kramer says!"

"Sick!" Gardiner laughed.

Three prisoners were led between them down to the cells.

"And another thing about Lucky—his shop is built so high off the ground it's possible he could see the passenger was ducking down and felt no immediate danger. Then he hears a sound, turns, and the shot gives the car its signal—"

"Okay, okay, I've got the picture," Gardiner said, handing his glass to the small black helper. "But there's a few things wrong with it. Fine as far as Peacevale goes, but there was

175

no way that bugger could have attacked from the rear in the café. I drew the plans."

"They've got them out now. Kramer's working on the theory he came in through the bog window and out through the gents' door under those stairs. I admit that once the car was gone I didn't think to seal off— Jesus!"

"*Aikona,* he couldn't have had time to grab even the small change and get back to the bog door before the coolie looked out of the kitchen."

"The lieut's thought of that. He could have stood behind the kitchen door when it came open."

"And how long did you take to come in the front?"

"*Ach,* these aren't my ideas, you know! That Mickey is now suggesting they'd thought of a better plan and that's why they came into town, to try it on an easy place first. He's just copying one of Kramer's old ideas, thinking it's smart."

"Still, maybe, he's got a point there worth reminding."

Wessels sneaked a look at his watch, making it obvious.

"I can take a hint, Wessels," reproved Gardiner. "Only it's you who has been doing all the talking and I came over to see if you'd save me a journey by telling Kramer something."

Wessels nodded, and shook the fizz out of his Coke so he could drink the rest quickly.

"It's just this: he'd better nail that other bloody psychopath quick so this lot can get some sleep."

"Who, sir?"

"There's no less than five Portues in with us tonight, all asking questions about the Munchausen. They were put on to me to hear about the car crash and the print and all the rest, but they keep on like they're not so sure we're just bulling them. You know—giving each other looks. It's not making them popular with the blokes, and it'd be a pity if we have to ban outsiders if this goes on."

It did not sound like a message that Kramer would receive sympathetically, but Wessels promised to relay every word. Then he ran back to the CID building in time to see Marais leading a very cool-looking young man about town up the stairs.

14

On the stool where Martha Mabile had sat, Peter Andrew Shirley now reposed, languid and unmoved by all that had been said to him over the past six hours.

Kramer had never seen a man conceal his feelings of guilt so completely. Even the innocent always showed some signs of tension as they began to attach wild fears to trifles. And yet that unconscious act of his with the underpants had shown beyond a doubt that the smooth-talking bastard suffered a bad conscience.

Prick it hard enough and the rest would explode in a gruesome mess of sobbed confession. But so far every dart of fact had bounced off.

Kramer, working on his own now, tried again. "You advanced your mother's clock before waking her, you advanced the girl's clock outside her *kia* door—you did this to regain the twenty-five minutes you lost while causing the death of Sonja Bergstroom by strangulation!"

He might as well have said by giving her whooping cough.

"You had the opportunity to retard both timepieces—and so nobody would notice you were twenty-five minutes behind the proper time, you made a long journey that swallowed it up in alleged stops. The truth is you drove hard all the way."

"Timepieces is quite a word coming from you," said Shirley. "I must tell my father that. He will be amused."

"What else will amuse him? The idea his son is a killer? That he used his mother to take the edge off suspicion by being late for a framed interview?"

"He will certainly rather take to the idea that anyone could suggest I'd do such a thing as you allege and then take no precautions of my own—beyond fiddling the *timepieces*—

177

to cover my tracks. Nobody interested in self-preservation could be such a fool."

"I see them every day."

"Oh, do tell me—where, Lieutenant Kramer?"

"On the road, in sports çars. Driving at speeds which are excessive without due care and attention, relying for their own safety on other road-users obeying the law and doing the right thing."

"You're quite a philosopher!"

"Uh-huh. It does seem to sum up the philosophy of a poop who kills a girl and then expects everyone else will do the right thing—only Monty Stevenson didn't bloody do the right thing, did he?"

"What?"

"It was his own lawlessness that first drew this matter to our attention, although it would have happened anyway in the course of time."

"How much more have we in common, poor Monty and I?" Shirley asked, once again as cool as ever.

"Not your semen group, for a start!"

That was badly timed. Shirley shut up and made no further responses of any kind until nearly midnight.

When Kramer remembered he was dealing with a possible liberal.

"What is your attitude to the Bantu?" he asked.

"They're people."

"I see. With feelings and all that, same as you and me?"

"So they say."

You could not expect much more than that in a police station.

"What if I now disclose to you that a Bantu is willing to give evidence that confirms the tricks you played with the clocks?"

Shirley laughed, making it loud and mocking.

"You think he's a stooge, then?"

"Of course, and I'm sorry for him; perjury is—"

"You don't suck up to the Bantu because of a bad conscience about what you did to one of them?"

"Your ideas are very primitive, if I may say so."

"The Bantu's name is Aaron."

"He can't be Jewish as well, surely! A Sammy Davis in Trekkersburg?"

178

"Would you like to meet him?"

"Love to."

Kramer rang down to Zondi and told him to bring the man up. They arrived so quickly it seemed that only seconds later the door of the interrogation room was swung open to reveal the pair of them under the passage's hard light.

"There he is," said Kramer. "There's Aaron."

Shirley swung around on the stool and stared without interest at the solemn figure in a cook boy's suit. Then his eyes narrowed slowly before opening wide.

"Him!" he gasped.

And turned to Kramer as if he had just seen an apparition and not a baffled old wog.

"I've never heard anything like it, sir," said Wessels, following Kramer back to his office. "He just fell apart!"

"I knew he had a bloody conscience, man. It was just finding the right way of breaking through to it."

"He seemed more poop-scared than sorry to—"

"*Ach*, leave that now. Tell me what all this is about psychopaths; that's more my kettle of fish."

Wessels repeated Gardiner's message, ending it in the office itself.

"Uh-huh."

"Warrant Gardiner also made a point about the gunman having enough time to take the small change."

"Which he didn't do at Lucky's," Kramer said, dumping himself wearily down in his chair and yawning.

"No, sir?"

"Got—sorry—pinched by some mini *skabengas*."

The yawn went across to Zondi, waiting for a lift in his corner, and then to Wessels.

"This was the first time they take the change," Zondi muttered, forgetful of the formalities. "Is it not strange? What was of no use to them—the small coin—was of use to us, however."

"Ja, that's true," Wessels agreed. "At least somebody has gained something worthwhile from all this."

With another yawn, he said good night and slopped off.

"Zondi!" Kramer said.

Like black lightning it had hit him.

* * *

The store up near the station, which sold cigarettes under bright lights until all hours, was empty of customers.

A car carrying two men screeched to a halt outside it and one man jumped out.

Kramer was lucky not to be shot crossing the threshold.

"Put it away, Fred, and come here!" he ordered the squat, currently unjolly man in the apron who held a .25 Beretta in both hands.

"Mother of God, don't do such a thing again, Mr. Kramer! This floor I just wipe!"

"Here! Move it!"

Fred, short for Fernando and then some, hurried across, while his family, who had been listening to the radio in the back room, peered out.

"Is there something you wish Fred to do for you?"

"Yes, tell me two things. I rang Sister Maria today—y'know, Mr. Funchal's daughter?—and she said Da Gama was running the family business now. On what sort of basis?"

"Basis? My English. . . ."

A lanky teen-ager, with a downy mustache, came over and gave his father a long, urgent sentence in Portuguese.

"You know what basis means now?"

"I tell my father not to talk," the youth said.

"Then you'll do," Kramer replied, snatching him by the scruff of the neck and running him out to the car.

In which his attitude changed as Zondi circled the other end of town.

"So Funchal's death made them suspicious, hey?"

"They say if it had been any kind of accident or a sudden sickness or anything like that, then they would have come straight to the police."

"And told us what?"

"But when they read that these blacks have already done the same in the township, and that a policeman saw them outside the café, they have to believe it. Then they read that the blacks are dead and no more investigation will be done, and that starts them talking again."

"Who said it had stopped? It would have if we'd not got on to there being a third—which was thanks to a proper print job, that's all."

Zondi, alone on the front seat, looked into his rear-view,

which was adjusted to reflect the youth's strained face.

"You don't answer questions you don't like, do you?" Kramer said, lighting a cigarette.

"I answer all of them, mister."

"Who are *they*, then?"

"The men of our community."

"And Da Gama's the one they'd be suspicious of?"

The Chev cruised another block, passing the mosque.

"Let me tell you what I've got to admit," said Kramer, earning a quick turn of the head from Zondi. "To us in this country, a Portuguese man sells milk shakes and biltong. But Moçambique wasn't one bloody big café, was it? Hey? What are you studying for?"

The India-ink stains on the fingertips showed up even in the streetlights.

"Engineer."

"Then you understand what I'm saying, don't you?"

"Da Gama—"

"Yes, what was he before, back in LM?"

"When was that?"

"Before Frelimo took over—Christ, you mustn't play games with me!"

"Frelimo," the youth repeated, as though tasting some irony in the word. "One day very soon after the refugees come down through the Transvaal from the border, Mr. Funchal brings this man to my father's tearoom and says he is the son of an old friend. He asks us to welcome him among us, for he has lost everything in the takeover. We are all very sorry for him and he seems a nice fellow. But then we are South African citizens, and so it is not until other men come from Moçambique that the stories begin."

"They knew Da Gama?"

"No; that is the very reason for suspicion."

"He was from somewhere else? Or are you saying that, in his way, he had a job like . . ."

The youth looked at Kramer and said, "But here the people know you. There are initials for them I cannot remember now."

Zondi was coasting in neutral, trying to catch every word and make sense of it.

"Secret police," said Kramer, and yawned again.

As the Chev picked up speed.

Sister Maria, in a pretty dressing gown, tightly belted, opened the Funchal front door to their knocking.

"I'm sorry to wake you, Sister, but my boy here has just made a report to me that Mr. Da Gama should know about. It concerns—"

"I am sorry, too, but Mr. Da Gama is still in Durban. He is spending the night there."

"*Ach,* really?"

"Is a Sister's word not enough for you?" she asked, with the same gentle humor she had used on the phone.

"It's just—"

"He telephoned only an hour ago—no, less than that; I'm so sleepy, I'm getting confused—yes, about thirty-five minutes ago, and said I was to go ahead with the funeral arrangements, while he organized it so all the managers could be there on Monday."

"God bless you," said Kramer and raced Zondi to the car.

"The Munchausen and step on it. If it wasn't through the gents', then it's something Gardiner missed."

"But, boss, that is many men he killed for this plan."

"Got eyes like a vet's. No problem."

"I mean, what we do now is maybe foolish. We run, run—when do we think?"

"About . . . ?"

"It does not at all tie in a string. Dubulamanzi and Mpeta—how does he know them?"

"Those answers he can supply."

"Are you going to arrest him on suspicion?"

"Uh-huh."

Zondi briught the Chev down to a crawl half a block from the Munchausen, then switched off the engine and braked where it stopped.

"What's all this, then?"

"The drunk kaffir checks first," said Zondi, getting out and doing his swaying, lurching walk, kept carefully from parody, down the pavement.

He came back on his toes, running swiftly.

"There is a light under the kitchen door, boss, and I can see a man is moving in there!'

"Hey?"

"And you see that car I pressed my hand on to stop from falling? That engine is warm inside."

"He's back, then!"

"Making the coffee?"

"Right! Any other lights?"

"*Aikona*, just the one. The padlock is also off the front door and I think it will just open."

"Expecting company, then. Come, we go together."

"And the plan?"

"I'm going to take him. You wait the other side and follow his friend in. What's the matter, man? Do you want to try for both at once?"

The door swung open at the press of his fingertips, and Kramer paused only to check that the feet were still in the kitchen. They were, and he could hear the clatter of a cup being placed in a saucer. When the boiling water was being poured—that would be the moment.

He advanced halfway across the rubber tiles, then stopped to listen. The sound took shape and he could pick out words being sung softly—words that had no meaning for him, as they were in Portuguese. Yet they gave him the final reassurance he needed.

A loud click came from the kitchen and the singing stopped. An electric kettle rang against a coffee jar.

In three strides he reached the door.

The water wobbled from the kettle's lip.

Kramer burst into the kitchen and jabbed his gun into the man's back.

Then saw the man was black and wore a scarf around his jaw as though he had a toothache. The dishwasher!

Who then attacked Kramer with sudden and terrible skill, uttering not a sound. Which only a faceful of scalding tea could stop before another neck was bruiselessly broken.

Kramer bundled the killer out in the café, registering as he did so that he'd lost his gun and two cups lay shattered on the floor behind him.

By then it was too late.

High above and in front of them, a rifle bolt was worked in a breech. A deliberate, alarming sound that jerked up the dishwasher's head in a splash of light from the street to take

183

the bullet right between his eyes. And level with the floor as he sagged to his knees.

Before the bolt could work again, Kramer had dived behind the counter.

"I will kill you," said Da Gama's voice from up in the darkened balcony.

"You have to," Kramer replied. "Don't worry, I understand."

"Police?" asked Da Gama.

"Frelimo."

"Your witness is dead?"

"Uh-huh."

Kramer had by then heaved the heavy corpse in behind the chipboard of the counter and made himself a shield with it.

Da Gama, committed to destruction and escape within the least possible time, began firing into the counter. The chipboard proved just thick enough to slow the high-velocity slugs down and lodge in the dishwasher.

Either way, it was a matter of time, and Kramer hoped Zondi would appreciate that.

Zondi closed the door softly behind him, waited for a shot to ring in his ears, and slid the bottom bolt home to keep whoever it was up there outnumbered.

His PPK was already cocked, so he could move without making a sound into the middle of the floor.

The lieutenant was obviously pinned down behind the counter, but he saw no way of safely reaching him.

"It's all up with you!' the lieutenant shouted at the balcony. "All up, do you hear? *Up!*"

A heavier-caliber rifle cracked out its first shot above Zondi's head, taking NO SALE out of the till. It would soon get its range.

"Up, up, up!" the lieutenant shouted. "You've got no hope left—no hope *left*. Do you understand?"

Zondi saddened at the thought a fine man should be going mad—then got the idea.

"That's it! *Right*, Da Gama, this is when—"

That bullet brought a cough from the corner.

Then the lieutenant's voice, a little croakily, began another string of defiant gibberish: "Stop! Stop! I'll do anything. I'll go *back* and say nothing. *Stop!* That's *dead right*. Go on, shoot, you bugger! *Shoot!* You have been authorized."

So Zondi shot straight upward into the thin floor of the balcony, grouping his bullets carefully, and keeping the ninth just in case it was still needed.

An act of thrift more than anything, as it turned out, because first there was a sharp, bouncing thud from above, and then a dull one.

"God in heaven," said the lieutenant, staggering across with his brains showing. "Just wait till the colonel hears what you've done this time."

Piet leaned his air rifle against the tree under which Kramer was sitting, and joined him on the grass.

"Tell me again," he urged.

"Which one?"

"Oh, any."

Kramer was not really in the mood for stories, and his leg, half encased in plaster, was irritatingly painful. Even after a whole week at Blue Haze.

"Tell me some jokes, then."

"Hey?"

"The one about Mickey."

"Zondi? He is a man, and you are a child."

"All *right*, I *know*. The one when Zondi thought Gama had got you in the head, and you wiped some off and said you were so clever it sometimes came out of your ears."

"Who told you that?" Kramer snapped. "Your ma?"

"Mickey did, when he came to help us with your suitcases and boxes. He also told me how you made him steer under the gun flashes, and how if you opened the windows then all the smoke would blow out. But aren't you going to say the joke?"

"*Ach*, man—you know it already."

"That doesn't matter."

"And it isn't really funny because the dead man got nearly all his head blown off by the one bullet—which is why you must be careful with *that* thing."

"Tell me again what that *skabenga* did."

"Hell," sighed Kramer, and then realized that his means of escape were nil. "The *skabenga's* name was Ruru and he had once worked with Da Gama in a special sort of police force."

"Like you and Mi—"

"Uh-huh. So when the terrorists took over in LM they ran away and came to this town, where—no, that's wrong. First Da Gama came here and bossed an old man into making him his sort of son because the old man—"

"Funchal?"

"Because Funchal was rich and funny, not in the ha-ha sense, and he was afraid of Da Gama. Then Ruru came and worked as a dishwasher in their tearoom. Gama and Ruru planned to kill the old man and then, later on, cheat the whole family out of their shops. Ruru was black, so he could go among the blacks in Peacevale and find men—gangsters— who would help them."

"Why?"

Piet always asked that question.

"What did I say the last time?"

"Because they were promised a lot of money and could see how clever Ruru was."

"Now don't ask it again! Anyway, Ruru and these two, Dubula and Mpeta, made a start by killing shopkeepers in Peacevale."

"Lucky?"

"That one your ma must have told you!"

Sensibly, Piet said no more and pretended great interest in a ladybird.

"Anyway, they finally come to the day when they think that Ruru is going to rob an expensive—*ach,* a place in town where there's lots of money, and he tells them all about how rich Mr. Funchal is. They wait in front of the shop, they hear the bang, and they drive off and dump the car. Then they walk back to where Ruru said he would meet them in an old De Soto. Now, they don't know, but this De Soto is their coffin on wheels!"

"This is the part I like best."

"Ruru has already hidden the gun—which was just a pistol with no telescopic sights—and the exact same amount of money as Gama will say is missing, under the seat. Then, to make extra sure we won't go on looking, Ruru also puts a centavos in the tin and has to mix it with ordinary coins so it won't look too—y'know."

"Obvious?"

186

"Uh-huh. Don't forget, just before the car came outside the—"

"I know that one backwards! Gama went down and emptied the till. Then he called—no, wait. Mr. Funchal was sitting behind his till. Dubula could see this and when there was nobody going into the tearoom, he tooted his hooter. *Then* Gama, who couldn't see underneath him, knew it was safe to call down and tell Mr. Funchal to look in his till. Mr. Funchal opened the till, saw nothing was inside, and looked up at Gama to ask what was going on. Gama already had him right in his sights where the hairs cross and—"

"Who is telling this story, you or me?" said Kramer, and cuffed his head.

"Ow, you big bully!"

"So there are Dubula and Mpeta driving out into the country where the hairpin bends are—it's not very far. Ruru tells them to stop and he hands each of them big wads of paper wrapped in rags and says they must count their pay."

"He is in the back seat!"

"Correct. And as they bend to look at the money—"

"Which is only paper!"

"He does this to their necks."

Piet got up off his stomach and tried to imitate the action. "Is that true?" he asked. "Would that really kill you?"

"*Ach*, no!" Kramer lied with a laugh, because he'd just seen the Widow Fourie approaching across the garden with two lagers, and this was her child he was corrupting.

"And then?"

"Ruru does what he's done many times before, and he fakes an accident so nobody will notice. Then he and Gama go and see what the Durban shops are like and—"

"Why didn't they have a light on in the tearoom when you made a big fool of yourself?"

"Careful, sonny! What do they need with a light when they're just going to talk and up there on the balcony there are all those windows? A light would have drawn attention to them, and it was their meeting place. You see, Gama was white and . . ."

Thank God. Bloody Piet had finally lost interest.

Then the boy looked up and said, "Is that story true? You know, really real?"

"Why ask?"

"Because everyone dies in the end and how—"

"What's this? More stories?"

"Ja, Mum—the one about the snake."

The Widow Fourie stopped short.

"Trompie! You'd tell—"

"The one about the snake in the grass, Mum, that's all."

"Thank heavens for that," she said, sitting down and handing Kramer his glass before smiling.

"Was that Zondi just now?"

"Popped in to see how you were—I don't think he likes Klip Marais much—and to say they're not going to proceed against Martha."

"I'll see you," said Piet, shouldering his gun and going off to the barn.

Kramer was following the line of a stout branch above his head.

"What's the matter?" the Widow Fourie asked. "Don't tell me my favorite tree has now got spitbugs in it?"

"No. I was just thinking: after all that, there would be only one hanging."

"Peter? Peter Shirley? But I say he's mental!"

"Huh! The law says he can tell right from wrong."

The Widow Fourie made a face at him and then drank some of her lager.

"Have you noticed about Piet?" she asked.

"What now?"

"He never calls you Uncle Trompie anymore."

"Uh-huh?"

"And you know why?"

"Because I'm the landlord?"

"Because I think he loves you."

"Piet," said Kramer, getting up by grasping the tree, "is just another sodding snake in the grass."

ABOUT THE AUTHOR

James McClure was born in Johannesburg, South Africa, and grew up in the capital of Natal, Pietermaritzburg. While working for three major newspapers there, he became a specialist in crime and court stories. After emigrating to Great Britain, he worked at the *Scottish Daily Mail*; in 1965, he became deputy editor of the Oxford Times Group of weekly papers, a post he held until 1974, when he resigned to devote more time to writing. McClure is most familiar to American readers for his novels, of which he has written seven. He has twice won the Crime Writers Association's Dagger Award. He is also the author of *Spike Island*, a highly praised portrait of a Liverpool police precinct. His latest novel, *The Artful Egg*, is now available in a Pantheon hardcover edition.

Peter Lovesey

The False Inspector Dew   71338 $2.95

"Irresistible...delightfully off-beat...wickedly clever."
— *Washington Post Book World*

Keystone   72604 $2.95

"A classic whodunit."   — *Philadelphia Inquirer*

James McClure

"A distinguished crime novelist who has created in his Afrikaner Tromp Kramer and Bantu Sergeant Zondi two detectives who are as far from stereotypes as any in the genre."
— P.D. James, *New York Times Book Review*

The Blood of an Englishman	71019	$2.95
The Caterpillar Cop	71058	$2.95
The Gooseberry Fool	71059	$2.95
Snake	72304	$2.95
The Sunday Hangman	72992	$2.95
The Steam Pig	71021	$2.95

William McIlvanney

Laidlaw   73338 $2.95

"I have seldom been so taken by a character as I was by the angry and compassionate Glasgow detective, Laidlaw. McIlvanney is to be congratulated."   — Ross McDonald

The Papers of Tony Veitch   73486 $2.95

Poul Ørum

Scapegoat   71335 $2.95

"Not only a very good mystery, but also a highly literate novel."   — Maj Sjöwall

Julian Rathbone

The Euro-Killers   71061 $2.95

"Well-written....the ending is sharp and bitter."
— *New York Times*

A Spy of the Old School   72276 $2.95

"This deserves consideration right up there with Le Carré and company."   — *Publishers Weekly*

Vassilis Vassilikos

Z   72990 $3.95

"A fascinating novel."   — *Atlantic*

Per Wahlöö

Murder on the Thirty-First Floor   70840 $2.95

Look for the Pantheon International Crime series at your local bookstore or use this coupon to order.

Quantity	Catalog #	Price

$1.00 basic charge for postage and handling $1.00
25¢ charge per additional book
Please include applicable sales tax

Total

Prices shown are publisher's suggested retail price. Any reseller is free to charge whatever price he wishes for books listed. Prices are subject to change without notice.

Send orders to: Pantheon Books, PIC 28-2, 201 East 50th St., New York, NY 10022.

Please send me the books I have listed above. I am enclosing $_____ which includes a postage and handling charge of $1.00 for the first book and 25¢ for each additional book, plus applicable sales tax. Please send check or money order in U.S. dollars only. No cash or C.O.D.'s accepted. Orders delivered in U.S. only. Please allow 4 weeks for delivery. This offer expires 9/30/85.

Name _____

Address _____

City _____ State _____ Zip _____